THE STONES CRY OUT

A Novel

Sibella Giorello

Revell
Grand Rapids, Michigan

© 2007 by Sibella Giorello

Published by Fleming H. Revell
a division of Baker Publishing Group
P.O. Box 6287, Grand Rapids, MI 49516-6287
www.revellbooks.com

Printed in the United States of America

Library of Congress Cataloging-in-Publication Data
Giorello, Sibella.
    The stones cry out : a novel / Sibella Giorello.
       p.   cm.
    ISBN 10: 0-8007-3160-3 (pbk.)
    ISBN 978-0-8007-3160-1 (pbk.)
    1. United States. Federal Bureau of Investigation—Officials and
employees—Fiction. 2. Richmond (Va.)—Fiction. I. Title.
PS3607.I465S76 2007
813'.6—dc22   2006027915

For Fred Danz, who told me,
"Some of the best gifts come with obligations."

1

The dead man's mother lives on Castlewood Street, in a battered gray house guarded by a mean echo of "No Trespassing" signs.

"Looks inviting," John Breit says cheerfully. "Good luck in there."

I don't believe in luck.

It's Monday, the Fourth of July, and the heat index refuses to observe the holiday. The morning temperature is nudging one-hundred degrees when I climb from John's air-conditioned car, and the humidity hits me like a wall. The sticky southern heat doesn't shorten my walk to the front door; nor does the expression on the face of the girl who suddenly appears in the doorway. She watches me pick my way down the cracked concrete path, her dark eyes hard as anthracite. When I introduce myself—Raleigh Harmon, special agent with the FBI—she turns without response. I follow her through a living room that smells of grape juice and stale cigarettes. Bernadette Holmes sits at the kitchen table. She is the mother of the dead man.

"Mama," the girl tells her. "The FBI is here."

Mrs. Holmes takes one look at me, Official Investigator, and starts sobbing. "What happened to my boy?" Her sleeveless housedress exposes large black arms, where stretch-mark deltas flow like sandy estuaries to her elbows. "My good, good boy, he's gone."

Two days ago, on Saturday, Hamal Holmes fell seventy feet from a factory roof. So did another man, Detective Michael Falcon of the Richmond Police Department. Both men died on impact with the sidewalk, but exactly how they fell—and why they were on the roof in the first place—is anyone's guess. No witnesses have come forward, though the police are floating a theory that's enraged half the city. Yesterday, the mayor called the Bureau, demanding a civil rights investigation. Mr. Holmes was black; the detective was white.

Lighting a cigarette, the girl with anthracite eyes lifts her face to catch a mild draft blowing from the air conditioner hoisted to the kitchen window. I sit down at the table, offer Mrs. Holmes my card—she doesn't take it—and express my condolences for her loss. Even when I mean it, the words sound lame.

Then I explain how this works: "I'll be looking into the circumstances surrounding your son's death and asking a lot of questions. Some of them might be difficult to answer."

Tears welling, Mrs. Holmes looks at me. "Hamal's body . . . it's all broken up, ain't it? My baby, he's in pieces."

Since the Bureau wasn't called right away, I missed the autopsy. But everybody knows rock crushes bone. When I don't answer, she sobs even harder. I wait, feeling the usual awkwardness that comes from being able to offer only silence, followed by impertinent questions. "Mrs. Holmes, do you know why was your son was on that roof?"

"Why?" Her voice turns molten with rage. "Because that policeman done chased him up there, that's why. He chased my Hamal to the roof, then throwed him off! I'm not sorry that policeman's dead. No, I'm not. God forgive me, but that man deserve to die, killing my boy like that."

Of course, the police department's theory doesn't go like that. They say Hamal Holmes, with his record of breaking and entering, broke into the abandoned factory that Saturday. And the detective, working nearby, spotted him and pursued him to the roof, where a struggle ensued. Both men lost.

The mother scoffs at the idea. "Hamal didn't need to go breaking into that old factory. Ain't nothin' in there. Place's been closed for years. My son was a businessman, you check it out. Good businessman. He paid all my bills."

When I glance at the girl, she flicks ash into the porcelain sink. "Are you his sister?" I ask.

"Wife. And my husband wasn't doing nothin' wrong. Put that in your little book." She points the cigarette at my notebook. "You didn't hear me? He was innocent. Write it down."

"I know this is a difficult time for your family, but—"

"You don't know nothin'."

Actually, this is true. I turn back to the mother. "Mrs. Holmes, I'll be the agent in charge of the civil rights

7

investigation. Call me anytime day or night, with whatever questions or concerns you might have. If you hear anything that will help the investigation, please let me know."

She looks at me. "That policeman killed my son."

"When all the evidence—"

The widow is barefoot. She takes four steps forward, the cigarette held at eye level like a javelin. "We done seen the evidence. It's in the morgue. My husband? He's dead. Dead! Dead!"

Mrs. Holmes lets out another wail. In a room beyond the kitchen, children start yelling. The widow hollers for silence; they obey. Turning back to me, she says, "You came here to help the cops. We know how it works."

"That's not how it works. The police are conducting their own investigation; it's completely separate from ours. We're looking into possible civil rights violations committed *by* the police."

"You're one of them," she says. "I can smell it."

I glance at Mrs. Holmes. She stares blankly at a small television on the kitchen counter, its sound turned down, with closed captions running across the screen. Montel, the talk show host, paws his bald head. The text announces today's topic: *I can't trust you!*

"Mrs. Holmes, who told you about your son's death?"

"I don't remember."

"Do you remember what they said?"

She shakes her head.

"Did anyone say why he was on the roof?"

8

"They said Hamal was dead. After that, my mind went blank."

Montel gestures with the microphone, swinging it like a wasp is loose in the studio. The audience applauds wildly. I look over at the widow, seeing her compressed dark anger, all that anthracite in her eyes hardened by time and heat and pressure.

"How did you hear about your husband's death?"

She takes one last drag off her cigarette. "I heard, that's all." Then she walks me to the door, wishing me good luck with a voice dripping with sarcasm.

It's no use telling her: there's no such thing as luck.

2

Still parked at the curb, the white four-door Cadillac has its engine running, the air conditioner blowing full blast. Special Agent John Breit is on his cell phone, the steering wheel pressing into his big, soft belly. He hangs up. "Bet they were helpful," he says.

"Complete cooperation."

His bloodshot eyes flick to the rearview mirror. I turn around, staring out the back window at the house next door. A sagging porch juts over powdery soil, and an emaciated man blinks into the midday heat, his hair an electrified mass, his eyes full of curses for the fancy white car with the fat white man tucked behind the wheel. Just below the porch, a small pink bicycle lays in the dirt, looking like it fell from the sky.

"I don't like seeing that bike," I tell John. We both know it means kids in a crack house. "Did you call the second precinct?"

"Right." He smirks. "First thing I did was call the cops and tell them to do their job. Give me a break, Raleigh. You don't think we've got enough animosity out here—on both sides? There's enough hate to last another hundred years."

When he pulls from the curb, the stick figure staggers forward. Spidery hands lash the porch column. I turn around, staring out the windshield.

"Don't look so worried," John says. "Child Protective Services just got an urgent phone call. Anonymous. But urgent."

"That's who you called?"

He turns right on Hull Street, refusing to answer, refusing to let me see he has a beating heart.

This close to the James River, sunlight offers a different hue than the rest of Richmond. Brighter. Harsher. The light exposes all the ravages of this riverbank south of town, worn down to abandoned mills and factories. The brick buildings stand tall and empty, like old ladies dressed up for a dying church.

Once upon a time, despite the South's formal rules of segregation, white and black families lived and worked here in relative peace, side by side in the factories and side by side in the asbestos-wrapped houses. During the 1960s, all that changed. Richmond incorporated the area, swallowing Southside and spitting out a weird netherworld of abandonment. That once-quiet working-class town turned into the city's dumping ground for industrial warehouses full of Philip Morris leaf tobacco and public housing projects that quickly turned violent.

But in recent years, Southsiders have demanded some change. Two days ago, on that fateful Saturday, six hundred people marched through here, down Bainbridge Avenue, circling Hull Street and cutting over to Decatur. They chanted and raised fists in the "Parade for the People." Near the empty Fielding factory, the crowd stopped beside an impromptu wooden stage. The six o'clock news would later show how the crowd swelled the streets, how they waved the angry signs, how Mayor Louis "LuLu" Mendant explained that their bad schools and vicious crimes and soaring unemployment were all the fault of white people and money—white people who didn't pay taxes and money the mayor needed to fix those problems.

"Millions are tied up in these old buildings!" the mayor yelled to the crowd. "Because white slumlords don't pay their taxes! That money belongs to you! And you! And you!"

The crowd hollered back.

And a woman screamed. Twice.

Even on television her screams sounded pitched to heaven. High, terrified cries that turned every head. But they all turned too late. What people saw were the bodies. One, two. The men hit the sidewalk with nauseating thuds, a sound like coffin lids slamming shut.

More screams followed that. And chaos.

Police reports and the newspaper claimed Hamal Holmes hit the sidewalk first, near the curb. Detective Michael Falcon's body right after, beside the factory's cornerstone that dedicated the 1889 building to Jesus Christ. With the medical examiner's report finding no illegal or intoxicating substances in either man's system, nothing justified their loss of balance. Except conflict.

Immediately, the city divided between black and white.

12

"You won't find witnesses," explained my boss, Victoria Phaup, Supervisory Special Agent. "You won't do much. Ask some questions. Pretend we're interested, then close the case."

"Close it?"

"Close it," she repeated. "We've never solved a civil rights case, and we never will. We chase down prejudices. It's nonsense, it drains manpower."

"So why did we take the case?" I asked.

"Because the public's paying attention," she said crisply. "We don't take it, the mayor files claims against us too. So make rounds. Take John with you for safety."

John Breit, the only other agent guaranteed to be available on a holiday weekend. John should be top man on the office totem pole, given he joined the Bureau just after J. Edgar retired. But John, as they say, has "issues."

Now, climbing out of his Caddy on Ludlow Street, John looks furious.

"We can split up. I'll take one side," I offer. "It'll go faster."

"Stick together," he grumbles, locking the car.

Every porch on Ludlow has full view of the Fielding factory. But half of these houses are boarded with splintered plywood, and when we knock on the six occupied row houses, no one answers. The last house on Ludlow is a half-painted white clapboard with a sign over the door that reads "Jesus Lives Here." I climb the stoop, hearing plastic blades of Astroturf squeak under my sandals. Behind me, John breathes through his mouth, his heavy frame already soaked with perspiration.

13

Black iron bars guard the door, and a woman stands inside the bars with the wide stance of a toddler. She is waiting for us. I offer introductions, and she watches us carefully, her rheumy brown eyes covered with the blue glaze of kilned clay.

"I heard the whole thing," she says. "Right here. I heard it all, start to finish."

"May we come in, Mrs. . . . ?"

"Miz," she tells me. "Miz Iva Williamson. And I don't know what that's a good idea. I can't be sure y'all who you say you are."

John and I hold billfolds to the bars. Miss Williamson barely glances at mine, but her mahogany fingers sweep John's identification. She bends, setting the strange eyes an inch from his ID.

"This belongs to a hard man." She hands the billfold back to him, wrapping her brown hands around his. "Burdens. You got heartache. You need Jesus."

John smiles politely. More of a grimace, really. John reacts to "God talk" the way allergics react to peanuts.

"Miss Williamson," I say, "we'd like to ask you a few questions about Saturday."

"Go ahead, ask me. Let 'em all watch. I'm cradled in the arms of the Lord."

On the Astroturf porch, in the July heat, I can smell cooked onions and too many cats, odors that hang on the humidity like clothes pinned to a line.

"We can come back later," John says, quickly adding, "if that's better for you."

"Man come to paint my house," she says. "Seemed like

14

a right nice boy. But he did me wrong. So wrong that I don't take the chances no more with visitors."

"We understand," I say. "What we'd like to ask is whether—"

"Sometimes you can still hear the birds," she tells me. "Some mornings I open my door, and the birds are chirping like happy children." She pronounces the word "chirren," the old rural Virginia way.

Behind us in the street, a burgundy Bonneville crawls past, engine growling. Driver is midtwenties, black male, red bandana covering his hair. He throws us a cool look, then guns the engine until his wheels squeal and the vehicle fishtails right at the Fielding factory. I write down the license plate.

"Ma'am, would you feel more comfortable coming to our office?" I ask.

"No birds that morning," she continues. "That morning all I heard was people hollering, yelling. Oh, they was loud! So loud that I just about closed my door. See, I keep my chair right there." She points to the patch of green carpet worn to burlap threads. "I stay put and keep my ears open. That's how I live."

"Can you hear much sitting inside the door?" John asks.

Her rheumy eyes click toward his deep voice. "You parked your car down the street, across from the Milson house. That'd be four-two-oh-one."

John counts house numbers to the cherished Cadillac. This time, his smile is genuine. "I'll be d—"

"And you will be." She wags a bony finger. "Unless you

15

give your heart to God. Tell him your burdens. He ain't gonna arrest you. He gonna set you free."

"I'm sure you manage fine out here," John says.

"Now, I'm not disagreeing with them folks, what they're saying. Ain't right the man don't pay his taxes. I pay my taxes, look what I gotta put up with. We need to clean this place up. This used to be a real nice neighborhood. Now we got all kinds of cock-a-roaches coming in and out all night. And I'd like it to stop."

"We all would." John sighs.

"Miss Williamson, what can you tell us about Saturday?"

"Well, I didn't vote for that mayor. Years ago, he come by my door looking for votes. Told me he was a Christian. But I figure he'd tell me he was Muhammad's uncle if it got my vote. I was thinking about that when I heard them."

We wait a moment, but she doesn't continue.

"Heard what?" John asks.

"Must've been near noon because my porch was under the shade. Sun was directly overhead. Like it is now."

"You heard the bodies hit the ground?" John asks. "Or you heard that woman scream?"

"Same screams I hear comin' from these houses late at night," she says. "People going down. Least, my guess is they're going down."

"So you heard the woman scream," John says, trying to pin down a statement. "And what—"

"You know how I know?"

"Know what?"

"That they're going down."

16

"No." He sighs. "How?"

"Believers don't got to scream like that. Believers got eternal life."

"Well," John says. "That's certainly a big help, Miss Williamson. Thank you very much for your time. You have a good day."

He's cooked. Ready to climb back in the cherished Caddy, ditch this hot hostile street, and finish his holiday with an ice-cold six-pack. Or three.

"That's what them screams told me," she continues. "People didn't do what they should, and then it was too late."

"Yeah, thanks again." John steps away.

But she raises her face, the strange eyes quivering. "We know not the number of our days, only the Lord knows. You can ask him, but he ain't gonna tell you."

Through the bars I slip my card into her palm, and her skin feels rough as pumice. I ask whether I can contact her again.

"I wish you would," she says. "I don't get too many visitors. Not the good kind anyways."

———

Finally back in the Caddy, blasting the air conditioner, John drives us past the Fielding factory, circling the block so I can stare at the roof. He won't get out. "We can't get up there without the cops," he says. "They chained the doors."

Nice try. He's not hiking six flights for a civil rights case Phaup wants closed yesterday.

Across the chained doors, yellow police tape hangs

in ripped fragments. At the street corner, the sidewalk cooks brown stains, the iron-rich blots soaked into the porous concrete marking the termination of two lives and the ignition of a racial fuse stretching back centuries. Graffiti sprays across the brick building: "Dirty Cops" "They Killd Hamal."

"Sad," I say under my breath.

But he hears me. "This isn't sad, Raleigh. It's pathetic. Here we come knocking on doors, looking into a crime *they* complained about, and nobody answers. Why? We're white, we're law enforcement, and we actually want things to change. Instead they kill themselves—kill *themselves*, Raleigh—with drugs, guns, prostitutes, while a blind woman lives behind bars."

"I'm just saying—"

"Go back to the office. Write up the report: nobody will talk. Then close it."

"That's what Phaup wants."

"For once, she's right. These civil rights cases just stir up trouble."

We cross the Mayo Bridge into downtown Richmond, the city vacated for the holiday. I glance over at John's profile and see the crimson veins that map his broad face, the rough topography nurtured by thirty-five years in the Bureau, two failed marriages, rumors of alcoholism—the only other agent with nothing better for a holiday weekend than driving around Southside asking questions nobody wants to answer.

"Were you always this cynical?" I ask.

He glances at the rearview mirror and says, "You'll see."

3

Richmond City Hall is nineteen stories of uninterrupted government dreariness. On Tuesday morning, I have to walk into the building for another eyesore, a bronze statue filling the lobby. It shows a disheveled man in a flowing robe, his mouth agape, eyes pleading heavenward. The engraved plaque says: "*Misery*, by Tom Korman. This statue is dedicated to stopping violence in our community."

When it comes to killing, Richmond is a horrible overachiever, ranking fourth in the nation for per-capita murders. Everybody has something to say about that, including artists and wealthy patrons, people who donate statues to the public square with the vain hope that somehow art can stop the killing tide. My years with the Bureau have taught me just the opposite: the most creative cities, the ones swarming with artists, are often the places swelling with destruction. Don't ask me why.

I find LuLu Mendant's wood-paneled office on the second floor, and the mayor stands, buttoning the custom gray suit that matches his smoky agate eyes. He invites me to sit. "What did you find?" he asks.

"I found out two men can fall off a roof in broad day-light and six hundred people below will see nothing." I describe my visit to Mrs. Holmes and the bereaved widow who thinks I'm reporting to the cops; I tell him about all the doors on Ludlow Street that won't open for the FBI. "You were at the demonstration. Tell me what you saw."

He frowns, tenting his manicured nails. "You ever protest anything?"

"Not with six hundred of my closest friends."

"You have to understand Southside. We have white slumlords who don't pay property taxes. That's all we're focused on. Nobody was watching the rooftop."

Even the local news missed it. When the woman's screams shattered the mayor's speech, the TV cameras whirled, winding up with nothing but blur. Then the two sickening thuds. And finally, pandemonium. "If we can find that woman who screamed, we can move this investigation forward. She screamed before the bodies landed, so she must have seen something happen on the roof."

He arches an eyebrow. "You asking for names? You think I knew everybody out there?"

"Spread the word among your constituents, Mr. Mayor. Let them know the FBI is looking into this. We want to know what happened to Mr. Holmes. Not for the police. Let them know this is a civil rights investigation."

He smiles. "Because if it's civil rights they'll line up to talk."

"Pardon me for being blunt, Mr. Mayor, but if nobody cares to cooperate, why bother with this investigation?"

"You still don't get it." He drops his hands and leans

20

forward. "They care. They care plenty. But this goes back to problems inflicted on people, on my constituents, over a long period of time. The wound is old. And the wound is still open."

And my supervisor couldn't care less. "That might be, but while your constituents are busy not talking to the FBI, the police are mounting an airtight case against Mr. Holmes. Silence only helps the police."

"I know what the police are saying."

This morning, the *Richmond Times-Dispatch* ran quotes from the cops, detailing Holmes's background as a prize fighter. The usual "unnamed sources" speculated that Holmes beat up the cop, then fell off the roof in the struggle. "When a jury hears Holmes was a boxer, the closing argument is a foregone conclusion," I remind him. "Thug throws a cop off building, loses his balance. Case closed."

"That your theory?"

"Mr. Mendant, we need statements. Six hundred people were there."

His desk is polished into a glassine wonder, and when the mayor pauses, running his hands under the rim of the desk, he seems to be enjoying his reflection. His voice drops to low, threatening purrs. "Nobody cares if the cop chased him up there."

"How's that?"

"What's of concern to me—to my constituents—and a jury comprised of my constituents, is the use of deadly force. Unnecessary, deadly force. It's not the first time some lily-white Richmond cop targeted the black man."

I give him a moment, staring at his upside-down

21

reflection in the desk glass, waiting until he's ready to hear me. "The law's pretty clear on cop killers."

"You believe that fine young man busted into an empty factory? What for? Those factories got nothing in them, that's why we had the demonstration. Breaking and entering? Hand me a thimble, I'll show you how much water that holds in a Richmond courtroom."

"Right now it's the only theory going."

He pets the beautiful desk again and stands, buttoning the gray suit. "Hamal Holmes was an outstanding citizen in this community," he says. "Go see his gym. Then tell me I'm wrong."

4

For more than three hundred years, the James River plantations witnessed man's great and terrible nature that appeared with equal measure. Back in the early 1600s, thirty colonists from England climbed from a tiny wooden boat that survived a transatlantic crossing with little more than painted boards and providential prayers. The colonists who made their way up the James River hosted America's first Thanksgiving, an abundance they dedicated to God before the Powhatan Indians slaughtered them.

Decades later, at this same location on the James River, Benjamin Harrison sired his political dynasty. Harrison named his plantation Berkeley, for the English parish that produced those slaughtered colonists. He grew his fields into abundant crops anchored by a beautiful Georgian mansion. But during the Civil War, the Union pillaged the fields. General McClellan's army camped in the mansion and burned the fine furniture for heat, and spite. Standing on Berkeley's riverbank and surveying the beauty and destruction, one Union soldier composed "Taps," a mournful tune befitting time and place.

It was during the War of Northern Aggression, as it's known around here, that McClellan destroyed most of the James River plantations. Determined to annihilate Richmond, the general traveled far downriver, all the way to Evelynton. That plantation was owned by Edmund Ruffin, the man who fired the first shot of the Civil War. Ruffin provided McClellan with a literal and symbolic target. Union troops salted Evelynton's verdant fields. When Ruffin returned from the Lost Cause, he was the proud owner of thousands of acres of infertile farmland. Carrying a shotgun into the barn, Ruffin wrapped himself in the Confederate flag and fired what some consider the last shot of the Civil War.

But one Richmond plantation survived unscathed: Weyanoke.

I pull my car off Route 5 and turn into Weyanoke's wide drive, the pea gravel pinging the car's undercarriage. For once, I'm grateful my government ride is such a bucket of bolts. My beloved supervisor, Ms. Phaup, kindly picked this white K-Car just for me, with its blue vinyl bench seats, temperamental AM radio, and malfunctioning air-conditioning system that only works in winter. Without a doubt, the worst vehicle in the office.

Yet the odometer works, and half a mile later, Weyanoke's mansion is finally visible. It brings back memories. Ten years ago, MacKenna Fielding hosted a debutante ball at Weyanoke. We were twelve girls with round faces, paraded across the parquet ballroom by our tuxedoed fathers proud as peacocks. Among us, Mac was the most celebrated. She was the fourteenth generation of her family to live at Weyanoke, and she was beautiful, rich, and more concerned with etiquette than genuine feelings. Everything a good Richmond girl needed to be to ascend the social ladder. Except this: the Fieldings had been branded by their ancestors. Richmond is not a town that forgets its history, particularly when that history includes the first Robert MacKenna, who married an Indian girl, and the fourth Robert MacKenna, who aided the Northern enemy, saving his own land through treason.

After parking the K-Car under an umbrella of oaks, I walk the herringbone brick to the mansion's big front doors. A black housekeeper answers the bell and informs me that Mac and her father, Harrison, are riding horses this morning. But they will be back soon. I am welcome to wait in the parlor.

I choose to stay outside, sitting under a tulip poplar whose wide shade saws an edge from the heat. And from here, I can see the river's oxbow break glinting in the sunlight. The first Mrs. MacKenna—the Indian girl—named this place "Weyanoke." It means "where the water turns around." From a geologist's perspective, I can say she was dead-on. How could she know that historians would lay claim to the symbolism, insisting the river's turnaround represented a family that switched sides, a family whose Southern belles turned and married Yankees, including a Union officer named Fielding.

"I don't believe it. Raleigh Harmon, under my tree."

I turn. DeMott Fielding's smile could melt the polar ice cap.

"I'm waiting for your father and Mac," I say quickly. Too quickly.

25

When DeMott sits next to me, I can feel the heat radiating from his skin. "They're riding new horses," he says. "It might be awhile before they get back."

"Your housekeeper said they left at dawn." It's ninety-seven degrees out here, humid as a steam bath—how long can they ride?

As though sensing my question, DeMott glances across the fields, where leafy soybeans creep across a sandy bluff. "We've got three thousand acres. Those two will ride every inch of it." He looks over at me. "You still living on Monument?"

A weird knot closes in my throat. The heat, I tell myself. Pollen.

"I'm just asking because I'm renovating a student rental on Grove Avenue," he says. "Right near your house. Why don't you stop by sometime?"

Down by the river, a soft breeze whispers through the marsh grass. A blue heron perches one-legged among the pale green blades. "Sure."

He waits. "Oh, that's right. You're FBI now. You can't socialize with people like me."

"I can't socialize with anyone. I don't have time." It's the truth. Or half of it. The other half is that DeMott Fielding and I go back, beyond his sister's debutante party, to a night made memorable for all the wrong reasons. Even after I left for college in Massachusetts, I still heard about DeMott Fielding; my mother sent the newspaper clippings detailing his arrest for drug possession.

Finally he stands, combing hands through his dark hair. "My father's no animal rights advocate, but he paid

26

too much for those horses to destroy them the first day. Don't worry. They'll be back soon. See you around, Raleigh."

I watch him walk across the pristine lawn to the English basement, the tiny door tucked into a hummock of land. He kicks work boots against the black iron post, a relic for tying up horses. Mineral-rich clay falls from his treads. He looks back once. But he doesn't wave.

Twenty minutes later, as I'm getting ready to leave, Harrison and MacKenna Fielding come trotting down the trail beside the river. Mac's chestnut mare shows off a plumy tail the color of taffy. Her father's horse is black as onyx. When he dismounts, throwing a muscular leg over the leather saddle, Harrison Fielding is careful not to graze the animal's sweaty flanks. He hands the reins to an elderly black man. "Thank you, Talley." Then he turns to me. "Raleigh, what a surprise. We haven't seen you in years."

Mac hugs me, then draws back, holding me at arm's length. "DeMott says you work for the FBI. Is it true?"

I nod.

"How exciting!"

"Yes. And I wish this were a social visit."

Mac's face goes slack. Mr. Fielding, his voice rich with the honeyed tones of Old Virginia, says, "We'll take this discussion into the house. Otherwise, I might confuse our conversation with the smell of my horses."

Weyanoke's walls are three feet of brick, yet a Confederate cannonball still managed to penetrate one side of the mansion. The hammered black iron sphere is a hostile souvenir from the Rebels who called these people traitors. Today, the cannonball rests beside a window in the sun-drenched parlor that overlooks the river. It's an odd counterpoint as we drink iced tea in crystal glasses carried on a silver tray by the housekeeper.

"Thanks, Connie," Mr. Fielding says. "Leave it on the sideboard."

MacKenna drops into a floral chintz wingback, fanning herself with a paper napkin. "Every year, I think I'm going to get used to this heat, and every year it gets worse. How is that possible. Doesn't that just defy science?"

Her father hands me a glass of tea. "Tell me what brings you to Weyanoke, Raleigh."

I start to explain the mayor's civil rights complaint when Mac gasps, "I can't believe those men died!"

"Sugar, it's six stories to solid concrete," her father says. "Nobody's surviving that fall."

"But it's just so awful!"

He turns back to me. "Raleigh, as I already told the police, I don't accept any responsibility for this accident. And I do believe this was some kind of an accident. Of course, I'm quite sorry it happened. Naturally. But we closed every access route into that building. I can't stop thieves and squatters from finding new ways in. It's an elaborate game of cat and mouse. But surely you know that, in your line of work."

"Right through thin air." Mac shivers. "It must have been so frightening."

28

For one moment, Mr. Fielding stares at his daughter, his tanned face bearing the indulgent expression of a man both amused and annoyed by someone he loves very much. When he turns back to me, the amusement is gone. "What do you need to see me for?"

I offer the mayor's view, that the unpaid back taxes are what's drawing crime and ire from the neighborhood, and that Hamal Holmes didn't break into the factory.

"Once again, the mayor boils the situation down to black and white. Literally, black and white," he says. "You can't possibly take him seriously, Raleigh."

"The FBI has opened the civil rights investigation. So, yes, we're taking him seriously. And the fact remains, those men fell from your building."

"Are you implying this is somehow my fault?"

Mac slips deeper into the chair's wings, so far back I can only see her long legs and riding boots. Her father pours himself another glass of tea, then explains how ethical tax evasion works.

"I own dozens of buildings on Southside. At one time, these were highly productive enterprises. I would like nothing more than for that productivity to return. But the choice is not mine. This city ran my businesses into the ground with its taxes and regulations. And now my empty buildings are under constant siege from looters and crooks of every kind—including those voted into office as elected representatives."

"Unpaid taxes don't help the situation," I point out.

"While my buildings are being destroyed," he contin- ues, "the city keeps raising taxes. Where does that money go? Straight into social programs that keep these people

29

from getting real jobs. Southside is Virginia's largest welfare state."

I'm about to remind him that the FBI views tax evasion as a big no-no when he continues arguing his case.

"Please tell the mayor that when the city begins protecting business owners, I'll pay my taxes. But until that time, I find no compelling reason to comply with extortion. Consider this my version of civil disobedience—surely the mayor will understand that terminology. And in case you're wondering, I pay the state and federal taxes, so don't bother notifying your IRS colleagues. I'm withholding Richmond's money because Richmond is the problem."

Mac jumps up. "Oh, Daddy!" Her boots leave a trail of dry soil on the polished pine. "For goodness sake, you're talking to Raleigh. She's our dear, dear friend." She takes her father's arm and pats him affectionately. Sunlight pours through the mullioned windows, catching the broad facets of the diamond ring that graces her left hand. "Daddy's like all the Fielding men. Always making a point. Isn't it tiresome, Raleigh?"

I finish my tea, and Mac escorts me to the door. An ebony braid points down her back like an arrow.

"Congratulations on your engagement," I say.

She holds out the ring for inspection. As a geologist, my best guess is canary diamond, 3.5 carats. The geologist in me also perversely considers which impurity turned the diamond yellow—iron? titanium?—and whether the rock came from South Africa or Sierra Leone. Mac would not want to hear about impurities. Or black markets. Or conflict diamonds. So I ask, "Who's the lucky groom?"

"Stuart Morgan. He was in DeMott's class at St. Christophers. Do you remember him?"

I shake my head.

"We set the wedding for early September. Here, of course, down by the river."

"Sounds lovely."

"DeMott is best man." She leans in, her voice a mere whisper. "I'm so glad that drug nonsense is over. He's really come around. You should see him."

"I'm glad things are going well for you, Mac."

"Good seeing you too, Raleigh."

I'm sure we're both considering the last time we saw each other. Four years ago, at my father's funeral.

"Please say hello to your mother. We think of her often." Mac opens the massive front door and squints at the noonday sun blazing across the lawn.

"Oh my goodness," she exclaims. "It's absolutely beastly out there!"

5

That evening, as sunset casts Richmond in soft amethyst hues, I park the K-Car on Monument Avenue across from the Robert E. Lee rotary. The great general rides his faithful steed Traveller south into bronzed eternity, both man and horse the epitome of Confederate honor and gentility.

Back when my great-great-grandparents built this house on Monument Avenue, General Lee's statue stood alone in a grassy field. That was 1900, and this was Richmond's outer edge. But other Civil War memorials soon appeared—J. E. B. Stuart and Jefferson Davis—and the cobblestone street was renamed Monument Avenue. In the antebellum aftermath, it became one of the city's most exclusive neighborhoods. The Harmons' three-story brick home was soon surrounded by even greater opulence.

These days, my mother lives in the big house with a boarder named Wally Marsh. I live in the carriage house out back. Tonight the house is empty. I carry a pitcher of cold lemonade from the kitchen to the slate patio between the two houses, where General Lee's noble profile is barely seen through magnolia leaves that haven't been cut back since my father died.

I sip the lemonade and close my eyes, listening to evening traffic thrum over the cobblestones. I wonder whether it's possible six hundred people missed seeing two men fall from a roof. Possible, I decide. But not probable. More likely, LuLu Mendant is right. An ancient wound plagues this city, an inherited devastation that visits even those who never saw combat. The wound is old, but the pain is fresh.

When I open my eyes, I see my mother standing on the steps just outside the kitchen door.

"Raleigh Ann," she says, "drink up that lemonade."

Nadine Shaw Harmon's brunette hair spirals from her pretty head. As she approaches the patio table, her silver bangles sing while her feet, strapped into three-inch stiletto heels, click along the slate. Her dog, a canine recognized on her license as Madame Chiang Kai-Shek, tags behind. My mother plucked the name from thin air.

Madame pants to me, then drops under the table on the slate. "What's in the lemonade?" I ask.

My mother doesn't reply.

I thought Wally made the lemonade. That's the only reason I'd drink it. "Do you want some weird side effect to hit me without warning?"

"I added a little valerian. That's all."

"Valerian. What does that do?"

"It's an herb," she says.

"What does it do?"

"It helps you sleep."

"You mean it'll knock me out."

33

"Raleigh, your bedroom light was on all night," she says. "You are ruining your circadian rhythms. You have to start sleeping."

I take a deep breath and change the subject. "Have you been at the camp?"

She claps her hands; the bracelets chime. "There was a woman with the worst skin disease you ever saw—like Job's affliction! But the Lord will heal her soon. By his stripes, we are healed."

After my father died, my mother attached herself to a Pentecostal camp twenty miles north of town. An odd, rustic place, Calvary Tabernacle is full of sincere women in calico dresses. They are good, generous people who believe makeup is a grave sin. And they have not tossed out my mother, who by contrast looks like a cosmetology dropout dragged over Dillard's makeup counter.

Reaching over, she takes the glass and sips the lemonade. "Oh my, there's too much honey."

"Lemonade needs sugar."

"Sugar will kill you, Raleigh," she says matter-of-factly. "You should have heard this preacher today. He was from South Africa, colored man, just marvelous. He told us all about that apart tide problem."

"Apartheid?"

"And he read from the book of Micah. Do you remember how much your father loved that book? He could quote every line."

I reach down, petting Madame's warm fur. When David Harmon married Nadine Shaw twenty years ago, he adopted her two young daughters. He treated me and my sister like his own blood; we loved him as our father.

34

And he worshiped my mother. Which was the only reason he shrugged into his coat on a bitterly cold winter night and walked to the neighborhood market. My mother craved shortbread cookies. But between here and the market, somebody stole his last breath, emptying their semi-automatic pistol into his body. Four years later, no suspects have been found.

When it happened, I was working as a forensic geologist in the FBI's materials analysis lab in Washington DC. Six months later, I entered Quantico and graduated to special agent. On graduation day, ten months after his death, my mother was still bedridden with grief, and the sky over the academy gathered for a summer storm. I walked down to the training ground, grass still moist with morning dew, and read the book of Micah, whispering the lines my father quoted all the time. It was a childish effort to will David Harmon's spirit to my side.

And what does the Lord require of you? To act justly and to love mercy and to walk humbly with your God.

I look at my mother, but she is staring off into the distance.

"Speaking of South Africa, the Fieldings say hello."

She blinks. "Oh. The Fieldings. Did Peery and Harrison go to South Africa?"

"No. I just saw Mac. She was wearing a diamond. Probably from South Africa." I try again. "Geology, that was the connection with South Africa and that preacher. Geology. Sorry." I try very hard not to confuse my mother.

"Well, isn't that wonderful news. Do you know the groom?"

"No."

"I hope you get married someday, Raleigh. Your father would want that."

The traffic winding round Robert E. Lee has slowed to sporadic bursts, and the fading sun has painted our brick deep purple. "I should head in," I tell her.

But my mother does not seem to hear me. "These hot summer days, they feel like weeks. One day is one week. One week becomes a month, a month turns into a year. Then suddenly I wake up, and it's November 29 again." She frowns. "Does this happen to you?"

"Yes."

Because she is watching, because it will make her feel better, because she's thinking of that morbid date when her world came to an end, I finish the lemonade. There is not much I can do for her; I take opportunities as they come. And when I ask if she needs anything, she shakes her pretty head. I carry the glass and pitcher to the kitchen, and on my way back across the courtyard, I lean down to kiss her cheek. Her skin is soft as talc.

She is gazing at the sky again. At my good night, she nods vaguely, waiting for stars.

6

Sure enough, the valerian-laced lemonade knocks me out cold. And for the first time in weeks, I sleep. Unfortunately, it's not good sleep. It's fitful slumber, a counterfeit version of sleep, like what you get on an airplane. When I wake before dawn, I feel grouchy and angry with myself for drinking that strange concoction.

The only good part: I'm first into the office.

My cattle stall—otherwise known as a cubicle—sits on the second floor of an unmarked glass block building off Parham Road. Most of our agent cubicles are perfectly identical. Only mine looks like a hurricane slammed into a paper mill. I will not claim full responsibility. Here at the FBI, we are a tree-killing agency. My desk holds evidence notes, interview notes, task force information, and plenty of FD-302s, a document that describes only what was said and only what's known to be true at the time of the encounter. Just the facts, ma'am. Reading FD-302s aloud is like listening to a jackhammer.

This morning's FDs are pretty darn simple. Because regarding the rooftop deaths, nothing was said, nothing new is known. Still, even nothing gets triplicate treat-

ment—life under the federal umbrella means three copies. One is my working copy, two and three are antic-
ipated trial preparation for the assistant U.S. attorney
(our side) and the defense (the enemy camp).

About the only benefit from spreading this much paper
around is that it discourages people from doing something impertinent—like using my telephone or, worse,
eating my food. I keep a lot of food with me at all times;
I am always hungry. So my desk contains a three-week
supply of munchies, along with a range of beverages
guaranteed to etch porcelain right off your teeth.

I'm diving into a box of Famous Amos chocolate chip
cookies as the big clock across the room reads 5:15
a.m. I wash down the sugar with a can of Coca-Cola
(never, ever Pepsi) and continue my computer search
on Hamal Holmes. It's not turning up much, except that
he owned a boxing gym on Second Street, had a tax
record nearly as questionable as Harrison Fielding's,
and drove a brand-new Lexus. He paid all his mother's
city utilities and her mortgage and received several civic
commendations from the mayor, LuLu Mendant, for
his work with young men.

When my phone rings, my heart plummets. I walk
to the elevator and ride to the fifth floor, the top floor,
the office of Supervisory Special Agent Victoria Phaup.
She is always here early, always leaving late. She trusts
no one.

She points at a seat with her pencil. "Update."

"I knocked on doors with John," I begin. "The only
witness is an old woman who couldn't read a stop sign
from six inches."

She nods; she suspected as much. "You checked the dead guys' backgrounds?"

"The two deceaseds are Hamal Holmes and Detective Michael Falcon. I met with Holmes's mother and his widow. They weren't much help and probably won't be in the future. I haven't gotten to the detective's . . ." My voice trails off. Phaup isn't listening. She shuffles notes on her desk. This has happened before. According to John, the source of most office gossip, Phaup ran the fast track at Bureau headquarters until she accidentally sent an email to the wrong recipient—in fact, to the supervisor her note criticized. Since then, she's bounced from one position to another, finally landing here in the Richmond field office, one of the Bureau's smallest operations. I watch her peel paper from several piles, looking baffled. Inevitably, her nickname is Foul-up.

"Here they are." She looks relieved, holding two pink message slips. "I got a call from *People* magazine. That's right, *People*. They're writing a story about some rapper who grew up in Richmond. He told them all about the roof deaths, how the cops here are racists and that's why he became a rapper. Now *People* wants a comment from us on 'the serious racial problems in Richmond.'" She places the pink slip near her phone. "Then, I got a call from the Richmond PD chief. He says nobody called him about this civil rights case. Is that true?"

"How informed should he be?"

"Touch base, Raleigh. But don't tell him we're closing it."

I nod, wondering, *How stupid does she think I am?*

"I should probably assign a senior agent to this case,"

she continues, "just to wrap it up. But I'll reiterate. We need this resolved now, Raleigh."

"Resolved, or closed?"

"Don't split hairs. Close it. Or I'll put John in charge of it."

Since I never can tell when these meetings are over, I wait to be excused. She's lost in her papers again, and I glance out the corner window. The morning sky is pale as quartz. Down below, in the parking lot, guards at the front gate examine a FedEx truck. When I glance back at Phaup, she's adjusting herself. I quickly look away. Among other questionable habits, my supervisor has a tendency to tug at her bra straps and pantyhose, constantly putting her undergarments in place. She reminds me of a nervous third-base coach.

"Call the police chief today," she says. "Tell him we appreciate his cooperation, we want to work together, et cetera, et cetera. Then we close. Understand?"

"Yes, ma'am." Taking that as my exit, I stand up.

"Raleigh?"

I sit down. "Yes, ma'am."

She shrugs one shoulder pad back into place. "Things at home, they're . . . all right?"

I should tell Phaup the truth. I should tell her that my mother is doing better lately. Sometimes even seems well. I should tell all this to Phaup, and soon I will find myself investigating fertilizer theft in Sioux City, Iowa. The simple fact is, I can live in Richmond—a young agent, receiving her first choice of placement—because Bureau headquarters honored my hardship transfer. I need to take care of my mother.

40

So, God, forgive me.

"Things are very bad," I tell her. "Really rough."

She purses her lips, nodding her disappointment. "Let me know when that changes."

"Of course," I tell her.

7

The River City Diner serves the best grease in town. After some Eggs on Horseback—two eggs riding a strip steak—I drive down Main Street to Ninth and spend fifteen minutes searching for a parking space near the Richmond police department.

Like some hasty urban bunker, Richmond's cop shop is backed into a small landmass. While the city explodes with robbery, assault, and murder, the police department stays moored on a postage stamp lot with no parking, even for the cruisers. I stick the K-Car in a lot that charges five dollars an hour and walk all the way from J. Sargeant Reynolds Community College.

After showing identification to the guard behind the police department's Plexiglas window, she buzzes double doors, opening a hallway covered with yellow tile and softball trophies. Next to a bank of vending machines, I find the pebble-glass door marked 102.

Detective Nathan Greene takes a moment to answer my knock. His office is painted concrete block. No windows. A room robbed of oxygen. It makes my cubicle look like a palace.

Detective Greene offers me an oak chair, the kind elementary schools throw away. I sit and explain that we've opened a civil rights investigation. "Detective Falcon was your partner, is that right?"

He waits, gazing at me levelly.

"Police reports say nobody saw Detective Falcon go into the building Saturday," I continue. "He also didn't radio his location."

When the detective leans back, his chair squeaks. "That man worked SWAT for eleven years. The only reason he quit was his wife worried. Now, he's dead. He died watching over a bunch of crybabies having a pity party. No, he didn't radio his location. He didn't need to. How long you been an agent?"

"Almost four years. Why was a detective working crowd control, on a holiday weekend no less?"

He shrugs. "Ask management. They pull us for every stupid festival out there these days. We even work night cop backup."

"Why?"

"Manpower shortages."

What a useful term. Phaup uses it for closing cases. "Were you working the march on Saturday?"

He shakes his head. "Mike pulled the weekend. I'm on night cops this week. And next."

I flip pages in my notebook, buying time, hoping he'll warm up. I try the novice agent angle. "See, I don't get it. He didn't radio anyone that he was heading into the building. He follows Holmes in there; I mean, why else go in. But he doesn't tell anyone?"

His dark eyes are cold tar.

"I know, I heard you say he didn't need to radio. But can you explain it better?"

"If he saw the guy go into the building, he'd take care of it himself."

"You know that for a fact?"

"Mike would handle it; he wouldn't haul somebody else into it. That's the way we work. We're detectives. We get things done."

I ignore the dig at the Bureau, which every veteran cop knows is one long food chain of approval for every minute movement. "What about the roof? What do you think happened up there?"

"I don't guess."

"Try it one time."

Detective Greene's dark face remains unreadable. I suspect he's very, very good at his job. "This is my gut feeling," he says, "nothing more. You got that?"

"Loud and clear."

"Mike ran after that guy when he broke into the building. I think the guy decided Mike wouldn't chase him to the roof. Mike wasn't in the best shape after he quit SWAT. He got heavy."

"But he chased him to the roof."

"Right." He takes a deep breath. "That's Mike."

"Keep going."

"So Mike's in pursuit, and the perp runs to the top of the building, far as he can go. Finally, he's on the roof and can't go any farther. So he fights. This Hamal dude used to be a boxer, you know that?"

I nod.

"Figures he'll just take down the cop." He sighs. "Well, you know what happened next."

"No, that's why I'm here. I don't know. And according to the ME's report, Detective Falcon never drew his gun. It was still in his holster when he died."

"Lack of oxygen to the brain." He shrugs. "We all make mistakes."

I nod, letting it go. "Can you think of anyone who might have wanted Detective Falcon dead?"

It takes a moment, but Detective Greene throws back his head and laughs. He laughs a long time. The sound bounces off the concrete block walls. "Girl, we're the grave diggers! Who wanted Mike dead? Every guy who thought he got away with murder."

I manage to say, "You work cold cases?"

"Tales from the crypt, right here."

That fact was not in my information on Detective Falcon. "He's listed as a vice cop."

"Yeah, he's vice. And I'm homicide. We started the unit ourselves about two years ago. Just us fooling around, betting each other who could solve old cases. But then, we did solve them. And people started calling the department complaining. 'What about my auntie? How come they ain't looking into her murder?' They complained so much that management finally gave us the gig full time. 'Course, that was before they came up with these manpower shortages."

I'm controlling my voice. "Judge David Harmon."

"What's he got to do with this?"

I shake my head.

"Oh," he says suddenly. "Relative?"

I nod. "My father."

He waits three beats. Four. Maybe five. His eyes locked on mine, the dark color shifts from cold tar to warm peat. "See those file cabinets?" He points to a dozen gray metal drawers running floor to ceiling like a battleship. "We've got more than two hundred cold cases in there, last count. This city kills people faster than we can keep up."

I write words in my notebook, giving my eyes somewhere to hide.

"If we had ten guys in here," he continues, "we still wouldn't catch up. I keep telling them, 'How are we supposed to solve cold cases when you ask us to stand around the Two-Street Festival tagging people for open beer bottles?'"

I clear my throat. "Did you work cases together?"

"When invited. But that wasn't often."

I ask what Detective Falcon was working on when he died, and he asks me whether I remember Marvin Dubois, one of the evil Dubois twins. Marvin and Martin Dubois controlled Richmond crime through the 1990s. They finally got prosecuted for murder and sent to death row, but Marvin—known as V—died in Mecklenburg Prison, choked to death by another inmate. Meanwhile, Martin, known as T, was executed this summer.

"Don't tell me Detective Falcon was looking for Marvin's killer."

He shrugs. "A cold case is a cold case."

"Those file cabinets are crammed with victims, and you're telling me Detective Falcon decided to find out which con took out a convicted murderer?"

46

He opens his hands in some kind of show of supplication.

"You'll have to do better than that," I tell him.

"All I know is when T got his date for the death house, Mike went down to interview him. Guy can't talk after he's executed. It was Mike's case."

"Any notes?"

"We're detectives," he repeats. "We don't file paper every time somebody decides to say hello."

Another dig at the Bureau. And I deserve it for picking on his dead partner. "He must have some notes."

"I can look around."

I offer my card; he reads it carefully, then hands me his. I walk down the yellow tile hall, heading for the police chief's office to perform diplomatic duty. At the front desk, the policewoman tells me the chief won't be ready for ten minutes. Which means twenty. I take a seat in the waiting room, which like the rest of the station, is more of that sulfuric yellow tile. Meager sunshine leaks into the room through high transoms above the doors; the golden light falls on an elderly black man who appears to be sleeping.

Detective Greene's card is still in my hand, its edges curling from my moist palm. I read his name; he uses his middle name for his first, *J. Nathan Greene*. *J* probably stands for some Southern schoolyard horror, like Junius. Sliding the card into my notebook, I notice embossed lettering across the back. I run my fingertips over the letters, feeling their relief.

To the living, we owe respect.
To the dead, we owe justice.

47

8

Hamal Holmes's gym is located on Second Street, between Leigh and Marshall, and when I climb out of the K-Car, a smell of baked garbage and urine rises from the sidewalk. Quickly I feed quarters into the meter and race across the street, where a young guy with bloody eyes staggers toward me. He opens his hand, and I drop the rest of my change into his palm, knowing exactly where the money will go, and knowing some pious attitude about panhandling won't help either.

Since no signs point to the gym's steel door entrance, I follow a flight of narrow wooden stairs toward the sound of skipping and slapping. On the second floor landing, the boxing ring fills the floor. Two black men spar, muscled bodies glistening with sweat. But the smaller figure leans against the braided nylon rope, trying to duck his opponent's punches without success. Across the room, some young boys pound speed bags and skip rope. The room reeks of oily sweat.

When he sees me, an elderly white man pushes off the ring and shuffles over. Gray cotton sweats hang from a stooped frame, but his handshake is bedrock firm. He barely glances at my ID, and tells me his name is Ray Frey. He turns to keep an eye on the ring. The heavy fighter continues to pummel the small guy.

"Watch his left, Mel!" Ray Frey's voice sounds like rusty chains dragged over gravel. "He'll take you down!"

"Are you the gym's manager?" I ask.

"Last week, manager. This week, owner. His left, Mel! What's it gonna take—him rearranging your brain?" He looks over. "Owner by default, you could call it."

The small fighter swings, misses. Covering his head with both gloves, he waits for certain punishment. The big fighter smiles over his mouthpiece.

"Congratulations," I tell Ray Frey.

He shrugs, the bony shoulders stabbing his sweats like a wire hanger. "Not like we got a profitable business."

"Fighters make money."

"Good ones, yeah. But this"—he tosses a nod toward the boys skipping rope—"this is just a glorified boys club. All those kids, they got mothers can't buy milk. Or won't buy milk. Either way, Mom ain't shelling out for boxing lessons. Everybody's scholarship in here."

"Is that how you met Mr. Holmes?"

He gives a short bark. "Child, I was running this gym before you were born. Hamal was one of my pet projects. That boy could've been number one in the world."

"Really?"

"Cruiser," he explains with an almost professorial air. "Not heavyweight. Hamal didn't move right with pounds on him." He glances over, as if looking at me for the first time. "I got a contract from Don King back in the office." Pause. "You know who Don King is?"

49

"Sure."

"Man offered six figures."

"Wow."

"Wow is right. Boy was ranked number five in the world then drops off the radar."

"What happened?"

"Up and left. Disappeared. Here I got this leaky gym and a Don King contract that would've saved everybody, and Hamal just takes off."

"Obviously he came back."

"Yeah, he came back," Ray Frey says wearily. "But a fighter can't be doing that. You gotta keep up the momentum. We trained again, but he never broke top ten. It was over, done."

I ask where Hamal Holmes went.

"Mel!" he yells at the ring. "You ain't got the sense God gave a jackrabbit! Ronnie, go ahead. Knock his block off. What do I care. Take his whole head off!"

Ronnie—the big fighter—decides this is a literal order, and with the grin of a demonic jack-o'-lantern, steps toward Mel. Rapid punches fly into a blur of red leather. Mel staggers backward, his long-sleeved shirt drenched with sweat. With what little strength remains, he feebly raises one glove. A gesture of pure surrender, heartbreaking for its capitulation.

But Ronnie continues to pummel, the creepy smile never fading.

"All right!" Ray Frey waves his skinny arms. "All right, Ronnie! You're gonna kill him."

Just for good measure, Ronnie throws one more punch.

50

"You make me sick," Ray Frey hisses. "Both of you. Get outta here."

Ronnie slips through the ropes, graceful as a dancer. Shirtless, his muscles ripple as he unlaces the red gloves and pulls them off with his teeth like a wily animal slipping a trap. He yanks off the headgear and jogs to the speed bags.

Meanwhile, Mel stands in the ring, arms hanging at his sides. The sweat-drenched shirt makes him look even thinner, even more spent. Ray Frey turns, watching Ronnie.

"Ronnie reminds me of Hamal. Hamal in his prime. If I can keep Ronnie outta jail, we might make it to the top." Then, raising his voice, he says, "What can I say, Mel? Guy's a killer. A natural-born killer."

Mel nods, the headgear bobbing. "I know." His tired voice sounds girlish. Slowly, he makes his way from the ring, removing the mouthpiece and listlessly teething the gloves' laces. He leaves the headgear on.

Watching him cross the room, Ray Frey shakes his head. "Mel's a good kid. He's just got a real bad home situation. It's gonna be worse now. Hamal was like a big brother to him. When this whole thing Saturday . . ."

Ray Frey's light blue eyes are obscure, like dull opals. Looking into those eyes, I can't tell what his reaction would be if I ask the question I want to ask: if the kid's so broken up, why put him into the ring with a guy like Ronnie? I let the question drift away. But, sensing my wonder, he answers.

"It's like I told these guys yesterday. Hamal wants you to keep fighting. Last thing he'd want us to do would be

51

sit around moaning and moping. Hamal was a fighter, all the way through." He sighs. "Most of them understood. But Mel, he's taking it harder than anybody. Harder than me."

"But not Ronnie."

"Ronnie?" He barks his hard laugh. "Ronnie ain't built like that. And Ronnie didn't like Hamal. Too much alike."

I watch Ronnie, a perfect physical specimen of ruthlessness. Every muscle on him developed like a medical chart, yet his movements retain the elegance of a tiger. If that's what Hamal was like, if that's who Detective Falcon met on the roof, maybe the cops are right. Falcon didn't have a chance.

"Do you know where Mr. Holmes went when he left?"

"He went to Atlanta to see Coretta Scott King."

"He knew Mrs. King?"

"Uh-huh. Then she poisoned him."

I don't know what to say, so I say nothing.

"Whatever fell into the trough, it went straight into that guy's mouth," Ray Frey continues. "God rest his soul, the kid liked to eat. We struggled keeping his weight down. And maybe the poisoning was intentional."

"You're saying Coretta Scott King wanted to poison Mr. Holmes?"

"No!" He's suddenly peevish. "She didn't even know him. He was delusional, see? But somebody could've slipped him something that made him go off the deep end."

"Somebody . . . ?"

"Somebody like the four fighters ranked ahead of him, that's who. Hamal would've KO'd any one of them. That's why Don King called, man knew the score."

Ray Frey tells me this happened in the summer of 1997. Though Holmes never broke the top ten again, he later became part owner of the gym. The other owner is silent, Ray Frey claims, so silent even he doesn't know who it is.

"After he up and left, my heart just gave out. Broke in pieces." He taps his bony chest. "Quadruple bypass. But Hamal kept the doors open. He brought the kids in here, and the city started giving us funds for community programs. We did fine ever since."

I watch the boys skipping rope. All eyes are fixed on Ronnie. He's clearly the rock star around here. With short, sure strokes, he hammers the teardrop-shaped speed bag into red oblivion.

"What happens now, without Hamal?"

"Depends," Ray Frey says. "His widow filed suit against the city. Wrongful death and all that. Guess you know about that."

I didn't. But it's probably in this morning's paper. Now whatever facts the Bureau uncovers will help her sue the socks off the city. Maybe now she'll cooperate. Maybe not.

"She's asking for twenty-five million," he tells me. "Unlawful search and seizure, some such thing. I don't know the particulars."

"Twenty-five million's a steep asking price, even for death."

"That's based on what Hamal would've made. The lawyer told her."

"You mean if somebody like Ronnie got a call from Don King."

Ray Frey's old face crinkles, his version of joy. "I'm telling you, Don King's gonna call me again. I can feel it. And even if he don't, we're gonna be all right."

"You believe the widow will win." What I don't say is, you believe she will share.

"Child," he tells me, "this is Richmond. These folks are gonna make sure the city pays for what that cop did to Hamal. That's how this city works. People take care of their own."

9

After hours slogging through paperwork and writing FD-302s on Ray Frey—not as easy as you'd think—all I want is to slip into the carriage house unnoticed. When I touch the iron gate leading to the courtyard, it's hot to the touch, a branding iron baked by the sun. And when I turn to close it, a black streak knocks me sideways against the house. I look down. Madame leaps frantically against my legs, pinning me to the brick.

Wally, my mother's boarder, races around the corner, calling the dog's name. Madame shoots across the slate. Wally sidesteps her flight path like an acrobat.

He walks over. "She's a little pent up."

Still leaning against the house, trying to catch my breath, I watch Madame circle the patio furniture, trampling the flower beds riddled with weeds. "What's wrong with her?"

"She hasn't been out of the house all day."

"Why not?"

"Because your mother hasn't been out of the house all day."

Waves of dread wash over me. Suddenly, my lie to

Phaup comes back. The ancient warning is always right: don't test God.

"I found your mom in the living room," Wally says. "All the windows were open."

"Who called?"

"The Bensons, down the block. I didn't want to worry you. But they said the music was loud enough to knock Robert E. Lee off his horse. Those are Mrs. Benson's words. It was a Mahler symphony."

Heat from the rough brick radiates through my blouse, burning the skin on my back. I watch Madame cruise the courtyard like a crazy windup toy. When finally I pull myself from the wall, the brick snags my blouse, pulling the threads. I walk slowly toward the kitchen door, suppressing an urge to scrape my skin against the rough brick until I bleed.

"She's in her bedroom," Wally says.

I look up. The lace curtain in her second-story window billows softly. "You want me to call Dr. Simpson?" he asks.

Dr. Simpson, a retired physician, makes house calls as a courtesy to my late father. But his visits can set off worse episodes. "How bad did she seem?"

"She recognized me," Wally says. "And she didn't accuse me of being a spy."

"Good."

"Then she told me to cut off the water in the kitchen because *they* send signals through the pipes. When I asked who *they* are, she said, 'The government.'"

Over the years, my mother's mind has cleared and clouded. During her worst spells, she believes the government is keeping files on her, watching her every move. This is why she will never know I work for the FBI. She believes I'm a geologist; I am. And I've checked the government files. She's not in there.

"Don't call Dr. Simpson. Let me talk to her first."

"You should get her off all that health food," Wally says. "I mean, what does 'all natural' mean?"

"Cyanide is all natural," I mumble.

"What I'm saying."

The house smells like old dish towels and wet dust, the humidity camping in every room like an uninvited guest. I gaze around the kitchen, but nothing seems out of place.

"By the way, some guy stopped by," Wally says.

"What guy?"

"DeMutt."

"DeMott?"

He shrugs. "Whatever his name is."

"DeMott Fielding. What did he want?"

"Beats me." Wally reaches into his back pocket and hands me an envelope. "I just got Nadine upstairs when the doorbell rang. There he was. Talk about Old Richmond. I bet he wears madras shorts for fun. He wanted you to have this. Don't worry, I didn't read it."

I drop the note into my purse, leaving the bag by the back door. While Wally goes outside to check on Madame, I wander farther into the house. The plaster walls seem to sweat with the heat, the humidity, and the big rooms feel tight as cupboards with family heirlooms. My parents never would install air-conditioning, much as I begged. They said they didn't need it. And provided you kept every door and window closed every single summer day, provided you didn't turn on any appliances, provided you kept every light off until dark—no, there wasn't any need. My father was the type of man who cheerfully pointed out how small daily challenges built endurance. Nothing fazed him. Not even my mother.

But after the windows have been wide open on a steaming July day, the old brick house grips the moist heat like an unexpressed sigh. I wander each of the first floor's nine rooms, mopping sweat from my brow, looking for something, anything to explain this sudden episode. Something to alleviate the guilt of lying to Phaup about my mother's condition.

In the front parlor, the bay windows are closed, the blue velvet curtains dropped. Pulling back a panel, I watch traffic circle General Lee and Traveller. Out there, everything looks so normal. When I turn around, I see a red blanket on the couch, some notepaper on the coffee table. I pick up the paper. My mother's square-block handwriting covers half the page.

Yellow chiffon dress.

She won't tell.

Mighty fortress of God.

The words run down the page like Oriental script, the sentences lined up in columns, so that the vertical lines create new horizontal words. Nonsense words and crazy phrases.

I walk up the stairs, the house closing in, warmer, tighter. Most of these rooms we shut tight, using only two bedrooms and two baths, one doubling as Wally's darkroom. The third floor stays entirely closed, holding my father's belongings; neither of us has the courage to go through his things.

My mother lies on the four-poster bed, the bed she shared with David Harmon for twenty years. She doesn't seem to hear me open the door.

"Mom?"

Slowly, she turns. Her black curls are unruly, her brown eyes unreal. Against such pale skin, her eyes are like shards of jasper set in porcelain. The face of a beautiful lost doll. "You all right?"

She nods. She nods the way small children do when they are hurt—emphasizing the top and bottom of the gesture. When I take her outstretched hand, her skin feels chilled. I imagine the blanket pulled tight against the summer heat, with her writing her crazy words into crazy phrases while Gustav Mahler hammers the plaster walls.

"Can I bring you something?"

Her lips are dry, white. "Tea. Hot tea, please."

Down in the kitchen, I boil the water, blotting perspiration from my face. Wally and Madame come in from the courtyard. The dog's eyes are darting back and forth as though she's preparing for enemy attack. Wally drops ice cubes in her water bowl. Madame laps desperately, splashing as much as she drinks.

"What's your schedule for tomorrow?" I ask.

"I have a photo shoot in the afternoon. But I can stay here all morning."

The water boils, and I take the tea upstairs. Madame follows, jumping onto the high bed and dropping down next to my mother. When I offer the mug, she wraps her hands around it, ignoring the ice I've placed in a bowl on the tray. I rub a cube against my wrist, catching melt with a napkin. Sweat beads the nape of my neck, rolls down my spine.

"What happened?" I ask softly.

She stares into the teacup. Her long eyelashes are coal black. When she looks up, the tears fall. "I'm a burden on you."

"You're no burden. Tell me what happened."

"I heard a voice, Raleigh. It told me not to go outside."

"What voice?"

"In the kitchen. It said if I went outside, I would get hurt." She looks into the cup again. "Did you use tap water?"

I take the cup from her hands, sipping the tea. "See? It's fine."

Her eyes search mine, searching for doubt, for any reason to believe the voices in her head over the daughter right in front of her.

"Please don't call the doctor," she whispers.

"I won't."

"Do you promise?"

"Promise."

We sit in silence.

"I think I just need some rest," she says finally.

I kiss her cheek and walk downstairs through the kitchen doors to the courtyard. The afternoon heat is so thick it seems I could scoop it with both hands. Inside the carriage house, I crank the window air conditioner and then peel damp clothing from my body.

When my knees hit the bedroom floor, my prayers have no pauses.

They also have no words.

10

Possession is nine-tenths of the law, even in criminal investigations. And at 8:30 the next morning, I'm arguing for that remaining one-tenth. The director of internal affairs for the Richmond police department, a man named Jeremy Owler, is unswayed.

"This is a pending case, Agent Harmon," he tells me. "No way will I release anything until we close our investigation first. The FBI does not take precedence over this department."

I try to explain again. "Just let me look at some of the physical evidence, whatever was collected from the scene."

He grins. "Tell me what you have, and we'll go from there."

This is Owler's idea of a good joke. In civil rights cases, the attorney general strongly recommends that FBI agents refrain from sharing information with the local police. We're investigating them, after all. But it's a bad double standard because those same guidelines strongly recommend local police to spill everything to the FBI. Maybe it all looks good on paper. But only a lawyer could devise such rules. It never works in real life. And Jeremy Owler knows it. He might be young—thirty-two is my guess—but he also looks like somebody who wants to run for public office. And nailing a cop killer is a real resume booster.

"I can't tell you what I have, Owler. You know that."

His smile ratchets the glasses on his beakish nose. "Well, then, we're done with this conversation, Agent Harmon."

A hard pulse pounds my head. I haven't slept since my mother's episode yesterday, and I haven't even eaten, a sure sign of distress. I'm desperately trying to avoid Phaup, who will ask why this case isn't closed.

"Just let me see the shoes." The pleading tone in my voice makes me want to gag. "Let me have some footwear impressions, so I can figure out who went where."

"Can't help you," he says cheerfully. "We collected the evidence, we keep it until Internal Affairs is finished. But, hey, good luck. We're really rooting for you guys."

Sarcasm never works. And when it comes from a guy who looks like a purebred weasel, it totally backfires. My mind flashes to those file cabinets in Detective Greene's office. All the cold cases, all the unsolved murders tucked away in a back room with no windows and one detective who can't come up for air.

"Owler."

He looks up, a smile still playing on his thin lips. "Yes, Agent Harmon?"

"The more you fight me, the farther I'll take this investigation."

"You don't like having information withheld? Now you know how we feel."

"I don't like your attitude. You seem to find this amusing."

"Not amusing." He fails to stifle the grin. "But I have to say, I'm enjoying holding all the cards."

I open the door. "Take a good look at them. You won't have them long."

11

My sister Helen stands in the painting studio at Virginia Commonwealth University, her thin arms gesturing like a ballerina, her long chestnut hair pulled into a hasty bun and secured with a chopstick. Grungy art students stand at their easels, listening to her pontificate about perspective. In the background, the sound system plays some modern pop dirge. The room smells of mineral spirits and unbathed youth.

When she sees me by the door, Helen's face gives only the slightest hint of irritation. She tells her students she'll be right back. Half don't seem to care, the other half look like they'll set the place on fire as soon as she leaves. She walks me to her office down the hall.

Dr. Helen Marie Harmon, Ph.D., professor of painting at Virginia Commonwealth University, has been teaching art for ten years, and any day I expect to hear she's chair of the department. Her big office glows brightly, the midday sun pouring through skylights. She closes the door that's blanketed with postcards of lavender fields and golden Tuscan skies. My sister travels the world as a renowned expert on Vincent van Gogh.

"You've got that look," she says.

I explain Nadine had an episode. Wally found her. The neighbors called. The usual, if anything about this can be considered usual.

"What kind of episode?" she asks.

"Stereo going full blast while she writes crazy stuff nobody else can understand. That kind of episode."

Helen drops into a canvas director's chair, where her name and "Ph.D." are printed on the cloth. "That stupid street of stuffed shirts. If they knew what was good for them, they'd just listen to the music. It might take the hair out of their—"

"Helen, they have a right to peace and quiet."

She waves me off. "And I have a right to tell them to bug off."

"That's a big help."

"Raleigh, what's the problem? So Nadine needs to release some pent-up creativity. All true artists are like this."

I sigh. "It's a little more complicated than that. Anyway, I thought you should know it happened."

"Yeah, thanks."

I watch her scowl. It's a striking expression on somebody so lithe and pretty, and in some ways only accentuates her ethereal beauty.

"I can't get over there right away, if that's what you're asking," she says. "I'm leaving for Amsterdam next week."

"Go van Gogh."

"It's a conference of international art critics," she says defensively. "I'm the keynote speaker."

"Congratulations."

"This is a very big deal, Raleigh. You might not care, but I'm a world expert on van Gogh."

How many times has she told me? As many times as I've wanted to reply, "You want to study a crazy person? Start with your mother."

"You want me to cancel the trip? I'll cancel it."

"Maybe you can bring her back a pair of clogs," I say.

"Don't be so self-righteous," she sneers. "You probably practice interrogation techniques on her."

"What's that supposed to mean?"

She walks to her desk and picks up some papers, pretending to read them. "Milky told me you called him."

"So?"

"He's my student, Raleigh."

Ah, she's changing the subject. My sister is a master at avoiding the topic of our mother. She's so good at this devilish maneuver that I've sometimes wondered if van Gogh's appeal is that Helen is secretly insane too. "Your student also happens to be a convicted felon," I remind her. "I can't go into details, but the only reason that guy is your student is because the Bureau picked him up. Contacting him is well within bounds."

She raises her chin. "I don't like it."

"I don't care."

She stares at me, I stare back. I know better than to blink right now; so does she. Helen's eyes are like turquoise, the way the color can range from palest blue to deepest green, all depending on how she holds her head. The awful music trudges down the hall toward her office,

67

the mournful voice of some rich rock star despairing that life is difficult.

"All right," she finally says. "All right, fine. Just don't bring me into this thing with him. Whatever it is."

"You're the one who brought it up."

"You should see his face when he talks about you."

Milky Lewis is a twenty-two-year-old former crack addict and the best flip we got from a recent drug task force. Milky suffers from an unfortunate stutter, and for some reason it improved whenever I interviewed him—which meant I became his main contact with the Bureau. But crack does things to a brain, terrible things, and Milky Lewis's brain started telling him we would get married. He even picked out an engagement ring. Eighteen months later, I'm still listening to guys in the office stammer, "R-r-raleigh, will you muh-muh-marry me?"

Fortunately, Milky had other dreams. During our interviews, he drew sketches of the people and places he talked about—for him, easier than verbal description. The sketches seemed pretty good, and as the investigation closed, I asked Milky to draw some pictures unrelated to the task-force work. I took them to Helen. After we busted the drug ring, Milky served four months on a plea, and for his cooperation, the Bureau wrote a letter to VCU on his behalf. Helen spoke passionately to the art school dean and pulled Milky a full scholarship—probationary—for art classes. Milky Lewis, who never made it out of high school, now attended one of America's best art schools.

"How's he doing?" I ask.

"Milky's talent is very raw, and it might stay that way," Helen says. "But it's also very real. He's transferring into sculpture."

"Is he around?"

Her green eyes flash with fury. "You're not talking to him *here*."

"Why not? I'm practically his patron."

"You're like the Gestapo coming around."

I sigh heavily. My sister's politics are so far to the left, Karl Marx couldn't catch her in a bullet train. But I suspect it's another reason she's cruising up the academic ladder, perching high among the egghead elite.

Opening the postcard-covered door, I tell her to have a good time in Amsterdam.

Her stony eyes defiant as ever, she lifts her sharp chin. "I will," she tells me.

12

That afternoon, I drive my mother to the Pentecostal camp near Ashland. We park in a grassy field where honeysuckle hitches the air and cicadas thrum away their short, happy lives. My mother's car looks as out of place here as she does. The 1966 jet black Mercedes with its red leather seats, all original, is a cherished family member. And it probably shouldn't be left in the blazing sun. But my K-Car is strictly off-limits to civilians, including canines, and Madame has come with us, riding up Interstate 95 with her nose out the window. The Benz has no air-conditioning.

The three of us—me, my mother, her dog—walk toward the tabernacle until Madame discovers a cocker spaniel pal and runs to investigate the twenty acres that comprise this religious weigh station in the middle of nowhere. Beside me, my mother makes her music, bracelets tingling, shoes clicking on the wooden boardwalk. I'm sorry to say she is wearing flats today, a bad sign.

Under the tabernacle roof, dozens of plain women in cotton jumpers sing and sway. The woman on stage is tall and wide, her thick neck disfigured by a softball-sized goiter. Raising her meaty arms, she praises God. The crowd cries, "Hallelujah!" Tambourines rattle. The organ takes off, an electronic riff harmonizing with the cicadas.

The woman tells them God is ready to bless them.

"Glory, glory, glory!" the crowd cries.

I look into my mother's eyes. They still bear yesterday's distance, as if all her sight is directed inward. Around us, people press forward, dancing to the organ, praising the Lord. I lean into my mother's ear, yelling to be heard. "You want me to stay with you?"

She glances at the woman on stage, then back at me. "Where will you be?"

I point to the seats lining the hillside's upper rim, a natural amphitheater leading to the fields, to the parking lot, to the dormitories that shelter these many seekers. My mother nods, squeezing my arm, and wiggles to the front of the perspiring crowd. I walk up the hillside and take a seat at the far end, out of the way. Below me, the ailing visitors perch in their chairs, reminding me of maimed birds on a sagging wire, waiting for the call to lay hands. Farther down, I see my mother's silver bracelets ricocheting shine back into the tabernacle. Her fingertips stroke the air like a blind woman reading the invisible face of God.

I've wondered what David Harmon would say about this place, about his wife coming here for services. After he married my mother, we started attending an upright Episcopal parish, his family church, redolent with Southern gentility and charm. The Harmons had attended St. John's Church as far back as the 1700s, helping raise the wooden rafters. We sat in the family pew.

But after he died, both my mother and I stopped going to St. John's. In my mourning, I realized the most painful place on earth is sometimes the church you attended with the person you loved. My father's absence felt more acute in church than anywhere else, an emptiness so vast that the hymns howled through my heart. I finally took a break from Sunday services, a break that continues without visible end. And my mother stumbled upon this unbound place of spiritual hope in the Virginia countryside.

My first reaction to this camp was fear: the people here seemed as off-kilter as she was. But the services appeared to quiet the voices clamoring inside her head, and the singing buoyed her spirit. It wasn't the place I would choose for her, but I saw the solace she discovered. Here she could sing and dance and shout for glory among people who did not care which pew she sat in, whose people she belonged to, and whether she was baking a roast for the homecoming brunch. These were people who seemed to yearn only for a pure relationship with that part of the Trinity sometimes neglected within organized worship: the Holy Spirit.

Slouching in my seat like a truant attending a matinee, I keep one eye on the goitered woman, the other on my mother. When the preacher lady tilts back her head, exposing her physical defect with such courage, I cannot look away. She steps down from the stage, moving through the crowd.

"God will heal any wound we offer!" she preaches. "Any wound, give it to him! He wants to heal you, he wants to make you whole again!" She moves down the

72

front line, preaching, blessing, laying hands. She reaches my mother, and her thick fingers wind into Nadine's curls. Cradling my mother's pretty face, she closes her eyes, praying fervently.

Suddenly, my mother falls and is caught by the people behind her. They gently lay her on the floor. The large woman continues down the line, laying hands, slapping foreheads. The crowd catches the fallout, moving around the fallen bodies like a river flowing over boulders.

I stand to see Nadine's face. Her lips are moving. And for several long moments, I watch my mother as she murmurs words I cannot hear.

13

That night my dreams are filled with an onyx sky dusted by quartz stars. I'm standing in the courtyard between the two houses, a charcoal mist veiling the scene. The goitered woman is here too, only now, Nadine is laying hands. My mother touches the bulb of skin, tenderly lifting the woman's face, calling on God to heal, to mend this broken vessel.

I watch from the side with my back against the brick house. My mother cries out with such clarity and conviction, a tone of voice I haven't heard in years. The heat of the day radiates from the brick through my cotton shirt, into the skin on my back. Suddenly, Wally holds his camera and takes pictures of the scene.

That's when I see my father.

His seersucker suit is wrinkled, as though he's worked long hours at his desk. He stands on the other side of the courtyard, watching Nadine. His blue eyes sparkle like topaz. I start to run toward him. But I can't move. I scrape the night air, stretching out my arms. The wall holds me tight. I try to grab something, anything to pull me off the wall. When I cry out for help, the women start singing, drowning out my voice.

"Glory, glory, glory!"

My father turns, looks right at me. Nodding, he smiles. Then he disappears.

"Hallelujah!" the women sing.

In my heart loneliness burns like a flame.

And when I wake, only the loneliness remains. My hands shake. My face is wet with tears. I glance at the clock, 3:33. Closing my eyes, I try to regain sight of his eyes, his face . . . his face shining with serenity, perfect joy. The first time Helen and I met him, we were five and eight years old. Helen later said our birth father never looked like him. "Like what?" I asked, because I didn't remember the man. "Happy," Helen said.

But the dream refuses to return. And the loneliness refuses to leave. I throw back the cotton blanket damp with my sweat, and pad through the carriage house, turning on as few lights as possible in case my mother should glance out her window. In the kitchen, I pour cold milk into a mason jar and drink it with the door open, feeling the refrigerated air ripple over my pajamas. Then I'm shivering; my clothes are soaked with perspiration.

Such a fevered dream. The kind of dream that will seem real for months, years. Forever. My father was here. But why couldn't I run to him? Why was my shirt stuck to the wall? The dream was telling me something. That I feel stuck here? I'm literally tied to my mother's house? But why was my father smiling at that? I can still see the way he nodded at me.

Suddenly I miss him more than ever. In the wake of

Nadine's mind crossing another trip wire in her head, I realize nobody is here to make it better. When my father was alive, her episodes were sporadic. And he took care of them. On a family cruise to the Bahamas when she decided the sea was calling to her; the time she accused the postman of reading our mail, of spying for the government.

I feel the damp cotton of my nightshirt, tangible evidence of my worry. Did I feel stuck? No. I want to take care of my mother; I genuinely begged the Bureau for this transfer to Richmond. The dream had another meaning. Lying on the bed, I let my mind wander over the details, still feeling my back against that rough brick, how it held my clothing like Velcro. The way my father nodded and smiled. The choir's hallelujah.

When I look up, the clock reads 5:18 a.m.

Behind the carriage house, dawn breaks the dark. I walk almost numbly into the kitchen to make coffee and wait until 7:00, gathering my thoughts. Then I call John Breit at home.

I ask him to meet at the Fielding factory.

Now.

Right now.

14

"Just take it slow, Raleigh." Peter "Boo" Bowman pats my shoulder. "Keep your feet on the wall. Don't look down."

I look down. My stomach cartwheels. Seventy feet of thin air ends with a slab of sidewalk. The faded bloodstains are still evident, morbid testimony to what happens when a body falls from this height. A warm breeze gusts up the factory wall, billowing my ponytail. I try to swallow; no saliva.

John stands next to Boo. "You really want to do this, Raleigh?"

I nod. But I don't want to do this, I want to run away. Quantico worked me until my legs gave out, but it never prepared me for this moment. The only people who train with climbing ropes are our SWAT guys. The rest of us stay on a need-to-know basis. And until now I didn't need to know.

Now I'm going to jump off the Fielding factory.

"Evidence bags with you?" Boo asks.

I check the two small packs attached to the waist harness. I've already collected soil samples from the southwest corner of the roof, where we believe Hamal Holmes and Detective Falcon struggled before falling. Footwear impressions are still visible in the black tar, but it looks like a disordered dance routine since the cops walked over the crime scene.

Boo says, "You've got enough line here to hit the ground."

"Bad choice of words," I tell him. "Really bad."

He grins. "When you finish your investigation, you can rappel to the bottom. How's that?"

Boo is our SWAT team expert. He secured one rope around the north chimney and tied a second—backup, in case the first rope fails—to the fire escape on the west side. He is an expert, a careful man who refuses to explain his nickname, though we all know it has to do with being brave. Still my knees shake.

"John's going down to belay on the sidewalk," Boo says.

"You bonk your head, all I do is pull the rope," John says. "Presto! You stop falling."

"Bonk my head?"

He disappears through the door and the building's stairwell. I wipe sweaty palms on my jeans.

"The chalk helps," Boo says, noticing my clammy hands. "It's in the other bag."

I shake my head. "Cocoliths will contaminate the evidence."

He stares at me, his blond hair blowing in the breeze. He needs an explanation, but now is not the time to discuss calcareous nannofossils in calcium carbonate and how they cloud minerals under the microscope.

78

When John suddenly appears on the sidewalk, Boo tosses a coil of rope over the side. I watch the rope free-fall through thin air and plop on the sidewalk with a sickening sound.

"You're good to go," Boo says.

I lean back into blue sky. The harness grabs my thighs. The rope slides between my fingers. Under my tennis shoes, the brick is gritty, unforgiving. And my heart thumps like a jackrabbit on amphetamines.

"Good," Boo says. "You're doing fine."

I walk down the wall to the sixth floor, grabbing the window frame with both hands.

"Don't hold the wall!" Boo yells over the roof. "The line will hold. Tie off."

No way. The brick sandpapers skin off my fingertips, but I am not letting go. I inch my toes forward, my hands creeping across the rock crevasses. Then I lean my face into the wall, aligning my sight along the brick. All I see is brick. It's the color of arsenic.

Still early, I tell myself.

Grabbing the rope, I tiptoe off the window ledge and walk across the building. Every fifth step, I lean my face against the wall, sighting for evidence. Nothing. Ten more paces to the next window, and when I grab the frame, mortar crumbles under my fingers, dry as burnt toast. The pieces fall to the ground below. I resist the perverse urge to watch them fall, instead dropping a sample in the evidence bag.

I keep walking, continually pressing my face into the brick. But, nothing.

Nothing. That view frightens me more than the bloodstains on the sidewalk. I walk all the way to the eastern end, far, far from the scene of the crime. Or the accident. Or whatever happened up here on Saturday.

"Raleigh! Tie off!" Boo yells, motioning for me to hook the rope into the figure-eight clip.

Despite the bloody fingertips, I feel safer holding the wall.

My mistake is looking down.

People have gathered on the sidewalk near the four Richmond police officers who escorted us here today, who now keep the crowd from swallowing John. One officer lifts a megaphone, barking. His metallic voice bounces up the brick. "Keep moving, people! Keep moving!"

"Don't look down!" Boo yells.

I turn, walking west. Sun shines behind my back, illuminating the craggy brick. When I lay my face against it, my right cheekbone stings against the baked clay. Worry bubbles inside my chest, percolating on the verge of hysteria. This was a bad idea. One very bad, expensive idea. And one huge embarrassment to these guys who agreed to help. To the Bureau. And when I'm forced to explain, fully, how I got this bad, expensive idea, I will have to admit: it came in a dream.

Creeping across the building, I start to wonder, *What was I thinking?* Early this morning, it all seemed so clear. I held my damp nightgown, recalling the dream in perfect detail. I could feel how the brick gripped my blouse like Velcro, and I remembered what happened the day before, when Madame flew out of the courtyard, knocking me against the house, how the brick snagged my shirt. The longer I thought about it, the clearer it became. My father smiled when my clothes stuck to the wall.

So I called John.

"I'm not closing this case until I know what happened," I told him. Thunderstorms were forecast for the afternoon. One hard rain could wash away evidence. Reluctantly John called Boo. And I called the Richmond PD chief, who during our previous conversation made the mistake of offering his department's help.

Now, well into this dream-inspired expedition, I had nothing. Okay, some brick and mortar, the roof soil. And a desperate hope that this soil wasn't ordinary dried mud from cop shoes.

Tiptoeing west, I start to pray, the kind of prayer that's more like whining. *Please. Please, let this be the reason for that dream. Please.* Passing a window, I see a wire mannequin inside, canting her hatless head with coy allure. A footless figure floating on a sea of litter. Right behind her, Harvey Guilder kicks through the trash, holding an MP-3. Boo brought Harvey. "Because if somebody opens a window in that place," he said, "they can slice your line." To which John said, "And I won't play Spiderman for your remains, Raleigh."

Standing on the first window ledge, I'm back where I started, whispering ever more desperate prayers. Down below, the crowd swells, and the megaphone grows louder. I do not want to look down. Or up. I stare at my fingertips, red skin pulsating with pain. Nothing is here. I will take nothing to Phaup and transfer to Sioux City to investigate fertilizer theft. Taking a deep breath, I close my eyes and lean against the brick. The rope tightens like a snake.

Finally, I lift my head to tell Boo the mission is over. And I see the one blue fiber.

The color of the ocean. One end waves in the warm breeze; the other clings to the brick. I reach for the adhesive lifts, my hands shaking with exhaustion and excitement. *I found it!* My fingertips are numb with scratches, so I pinch the plastic sheets between thumb and index finger. Here is one fiber for the lab. My dream vindicated. I pull the clear sheet apart, revealing the sticky side, when the wind blows up the building. It snatches the plastic from my fingers, and I watch the sheets float up then tumble through the air. They flutter like fat confetti. I look past them to John. From here his face looks pinched.

"What are you doing!" he yells up the building.

"Hold the rope!" I yell back.

People are pointing at the plastic sheets falling on them. Picking up each piece, they turn them over, searching for messages. Finding none, they look up, even more upset.

"How much longer, Raleigh?"

Boo is directly above me, the clear sky framing his corn-silk hair.

"You got any Scotch tape?" I ask.

"What?"

"Tape! I need tape!"

He walks away, then sends a metal clip with one white circle whizzing down the rope. First Aid tape. "It's all I've got." Eight feet from me, he's crammed into the corner of the roof.

"Fifteen minutes," I tell him.

82

"Five. It's ugly down there."

I move the rope to the other side of my face, then realize in my excitement I tied off, freeing both hands. I pry tape from the white roll and lay a swatch over the blue fiber, then yank it off the brick. Somebody in the lab will complain about this tape. But I don't care. I have evidence. My father told me the truth. Again.

Just above my head, the building's elaborate capstone rises in a graduated herringbone pattern.

"Boo," I yell toward the roof. "How do I get up there?"

He leans over the wall. "You wanted to go down. We need different equipment for up."

"Three feet."

"What d'you weigh?"

"One fifteen."

He reaches for the rope, telling me to start walking. When he pulls, I shove my bloody fingertips into the mortar crevices, my shoulders spasming with exhaustion. We get two feet, placing me at the bottom of the hollow capstone. I press my forehead against the brick. More dark blue fibers wave from the craggy surface. I thank God, twice, maybe three times, and toss four tape swatches into the evidence bag. When I scan the brick again, I find a curly black fiber snaking through the red aggregate like a dark worm. Human hair, I'm almost certain.

"How much longer, Raleigh?" Boo asks.

"Sure, we can come back another time."

"John's about to have a stroke."

"You got a flashlight?" I ask.

He clips a small light to the rope and sends it down. "Hurry."

I shine light into the cavity, waiting for my vision to adjust to the crevice's darkness. There's a bird's nest in back, twigs and moss scattered around. I move the light forward inch by inch. Thick, red fibers. I set the flashlight inside the cavity, take the samples, and tell Boo to pull me up.

He shakes his head. "It's safer if you rappel down."

My shoulders throb, my hands are raw. The crowd wants to kill me.

"Walk to the bottom, Raleigh. Harvey's packing up the equipment. We'll meet you and John below."

Giddy joy kicked to the curb by sudden fear. I walk down the west side of the factory, feeling the rope's smooth weave between my stinging hands. John's voice rises to my ears, urgent above the hollering crowd. "Come on, Raleigh!"

When I step onto the sidewalk, my legs are wobbly. And my fingers are fumbling with the rope. John shoves my hands out of the way. The megaphone barks commands, the same command over and over. "Stand back from the door! Stand back from the door!" Breathing like a locomotive, John wraps the rope around his elbow and shoulder. Slowly I unclip the evidence bags and I turn around.

Crowds make me nervous. All crowds. But to this crowd we are the enemy, come to persecute the dead. And we're with cops.

"We're the next flights off that roof!" John yells.

The factory's double doors burst open, and Boo and

84

Harvey run with that bulky efficiency of SWAT guys. The crowd closes in as we huddle on the sidewalk. John holds the rope, Boo and Harvey shoulder equipment. I clutch the evidence bags like newborns.

"Harvey, in front," Boo directs. "We make one line and head for the cruisers. John, Raleigh, in the first car. We'll take the backup. Do not stop moving!"

"Get back! Get back! Get back!" the megaphone screeches. We form our line, Harvey the prow, slicing this sea that would swallow us whole. Cradling evidence in my arms, I feel John's heavy hand on my left shoulder, his fingers tightening. Keeping my head down, I hunch over the bags as hands fly in front of my face. And the words, ugly words, land in my ears. I spot a blue uniform, a cop beside the cruiser with one hand on the door. The other hand is flung behind him in a futile attempt at crowd control. Sibilant and cruel, the words slip into my ears. Something strikes my face. Slimy, warm, it slides down my cheek. I want to wipe it off but can't let go of the evidence. Dipping my cheek, I rub my shoulder against my face. John yells, "What's the matter with you people?" The cruiser door opens, and I duck inside, tossing the evidence bags and wiping my T-shirt across my face. John's weight hits the vinyl bench seat. The door slams.

My face stings, but I rub and rub with my shirt. And suddenly the top of my head opens, as though my scalp were peeling back. My brain feels carbonated, all my thoughts floating out into the hot summer air. Thought bubbles. I am a cartoon scrubbing my raw face. When I hear laughter it sounds strange, nothing like my real laugh.

"You think this is funny?" John turns.

I shake my head. No. Not funny. Closing my eyes, I tell myself to breathe, calm down. I've reacted like this before, stressed into an inappropriate response. It's the character defect, the utter failure, of someone who bottles her emotions.

When the cruiser finally lurches, I open my eyes. Bouncing fists cover the windshield, then recede to either side of the car. The siren squawks. John stares straight ahead, and I gaze out the side window as Southside moves past us in a wake of despair.

Within minutes, we are crossing the Mayo Bridge into downtown Richmond. The atmosphere in the car changes.

"You okay," John says.

It's not a question. Not an inquiry. It's an order. The man's been with the Bureau more than thirty years, he's not the indulgent type. It's a statement: you are okay.

I nod.

But deep inside, I'm still floating around the edges, feeling like a handful of dry silt cast over cold water before sinking to the bottom. "I owe you," I tell him.

"No, you owe me about three hundred times over," he says. "And the person you really ought to thank is Boo. I didn't want to do this, he did. He jumped at the chance."

I nod again.

"So what did you find up there?" he asks.

The cops glance at each other across the front seat, then casually look out their side windows into the mirrors.

"You never know until the lab checks it out. Maybe nothing."

Catching my drift, he changes the subject. "You should see your face." Now he's laughing. Really laughing.

"You think this is funny?"

"Yeah," he grins. "But let me ask you something. Are you hungry?"

I tell him what he wants to hear. I'm always hungry. He leans forward, talking through the metal cage to the cops. "This girl. I wish I could eat like her and stay so thin. Unbelievable. She eats a couple hamburgers for lunch then asks what's for dinner."

They laugh. I smile. My face burns.

We pull into the office off Parham Road, and the guards open the gate. At the front door, John climbs out. I thank the officers for their help.

The driver's eyes are opalescent, rimmed with short dark lashes. He wants to know, and he doesn't. Like all his brothers in arms, the only answer he wants is this: innocent. The cops are innocent.

"Thanks for your help," I tell him.

He cocks his thumb and forefinger into the shape of a pistol, pointing at me. "Be careful, kiddo."

15

In Virginia, the Appalachian Mountains sinew like blue-backed caterpillars, all their soft folds and rounded edges looking gentle as a cradle that dips toward the Shenandoah Valley with maternal abundance.

But long ago, these same hills soared to heaven at Himalayan heights. The geologic cycle at its simplest, and most elegant, is grinding glaciers, rushing water, and whipping winds that erode peaks into rolling hills. In this case those destructive forces swept rock, sand, and silt to the east, filling a shallow sea and creating high cliffs along the Atlantic Ocean.

Today, you can stand below the sandstone cliffs bordering the Chesapeake Bay and find pieces of the Appalachian Mountains from more than two hundred miles away. Cemented by time, all that mountain detritus has become narrow hue-shifting layers laid down as patiently, as evenly as pages in a book. Because clams lived in that former shallow sea, you can see their fossilized remains too, white carcasses punctuating the narrow pages of dirt as though every typewriter in the world erupted the letter *C*.

My mother doesn't care for talk about millions of years; she takes comfort in 6 days. Most geologists mock 6 days, insisting that God (if he even exists) couldn't create heaven and earth in 144 hours. I used to camp between the two poles, waiting for more nuanced explanations. But I finally came to a couple conclusions. Honest scientists will admit that theories like evolution and the big bang are simply the best guess at the moment; good guesses, but guesses nonetheless. And I will never be able to prove 6 days. Not this side of heaven. All theories, not just creationism, require faith.

And science will provide as many questions as answers. Jonathan Edwards studied spiders to find out how they spin webs and came away realizing "the exuberant goodness of the Creator." Look around, witness the marvels. Track one piece of gravel in a riverbed all the way back to its magma beginnings, and then try to say the divine toolbox does not contain some significant wrenches. Earthquakes, volcanic eruptions, meteors, floods, tsunamis—the list goes on, with rising magnitude. Six days? Why not. He's certainly capable of it.

On Friday afternoon, as I drive up Interstate 95 to Washington, the dramatic cliffs along the Rappahannock River beg for explanations. But nobody cares. Traffic is heavy, and when I take the D Street exit, I have to navigate the city by hitting the brakes more than the gas. At the intersection of E and 9th streets, I pull into the parking garage and slide my identification card through an electronic eye to lift the thick metal grate. Driving under the FBI headquarters, I park and take the elevator to the third floor, then clear two more electronic eyes to get into the Materials Analysis unit.

Of the Bureau's forensics departments, mineralogy is the least known. The lab's two small rooms are located in back, past the paint chips guys and the duct tape experts and the much-quoted-in-*USA-Today* hairs and fibers scientists who grab all the forensics glory. But mineralogy covers more ground than all of them, literally. We're there for diamonds, dust, granite, marble, sheet rock, and seashells, to name just a few. Some years ago, when a sniper took a shot at the White House, mineralogy was called in. Glass is made of silica. By studying the mineral's fractured angles, we could pinpoint the exact location of the shooter who stood on Pennsylvania Avenue hoping to kill the president.

Mineralogy also took me places I didn't want to go. My first case for the lab involved a pair of lungs so small they were unrecognizable. The local PD's homicide report said they once belonged to a girl named Ellie Mullins, age three. Her body was discovered under a slag heap by some West Virginia miners. I found soil in her lungs, so much soil that Ellie Mullins's air sacs were near bursting. It meant the girl had inhaled the soil. It meant somebody had buried her alive.

After that first case, I called my father, wondering if I was cut out for this work. I wanted to study rocks and minerals, but I didn't want to think about how a little girl was buried alive, choked to death on dirt and coal dust. My father listened patiently. Finally he said, "I don't always enjoy being a judge, Raleigh. Some cases never let you forget the gruesome details. But I believe we're called to live beyond our fears. The work you're doing won't be easy. But the stones cry out. And the only way to get the answers is to listen to the cries."

So I stayed. I stayed until his murder. Until Richmond called with even greater cries.

Now, standing in the doorway of the lab, I watch Eric Duncan hover over a polarized light microscope. Kerr's *Optical Mineralogy* textbook is open on his desk. Afternoon sunlight cuts into the room through the north window as Eric's left hand twists the magnification dial. His fingers palsy, he shakes his hand as though flinging water.

At my knock, he turns, his freckled face smiling. Just as quickly, the smile disappears. "Raleigh, what happened to your face?"

I touch my cheekbones with fingers covered with Band-Aids. I hand him the box of evidence.

"You shouldn't have," he says, digging his heels into the white linoleum, rolling his chair to the desk and signing the chain of custody forms. He opens each film canister of soil and initials them with *ZG*. Lab techs never use their real initials, which are identical for different people, and can betray a technician's anonymity. With more mentally unstable criminals filing Freedom of Information Acts, the last thing we want is names attached to the guilty verdict.

But Eric's *ZG* looks strange. Backward *S*, drunken *C*. He uses both hands to snap the Sharpie closed. "Let me guess. You brought me some thrilling concrete block."

I'm insulted. "It's not *that* bad."

"Glass fragments. No, wait, *safety* glass fragments."

91

I shake my head. "Think of Richmond."

"Cobblestones?"

"You're warm."

"Brick."

"Bingo. And some mortar."

"Wonderful," he says without any trace of enthusiasm. "I see your Q here. No K?"

Q stands for Question—what is this stuff, where did it come from? K stands for Comparison. For instance: Soil K1 comes from the scene of the crime, and Soil K2 from the suspect's home—do they match? But I don't have any comparison samples because the police won't release the evidence. "I'll get you Ks later. What I need now is the mineral composition of the brick, and the mineral composition of the roof soil. Then I need to know where the soil might come from."

"Provenance," he says.

"I don't use them fancy words no more." When I smile, the skin on my face screams with pain.

"You look terrible," he says.

"Thanks. How long for the report?"

He pulls up the backlog, his neck muscles twitching. "Guess what I got from Iowa yesterday." Eric likes guessing games, probably because his work leaves no room for guessing.

"Farmer Brown's dirt."

"The local PD wants us to examine tires from a 1993 Chevy truck. Why? Did the car transport a kidnapping? Did the driver bludgeon somebody to death?"

"No."

"*No* is the correct answer—tell the girl what she's won,

Johnny! No, the police suspect this guy drove all over their high school football field. They're loaded for bear and sent us all four wheels along with fifty Ks—fifty comparisons from one football field!"

Once upon a time, Eric Duncan applied to Quantico. He got in too. Then one morning, his left arm wouldn't work. He couldn't keep shampoo out of his eyes. By week's end, doctors diagnosed early stage multiple sclerosis, and Eric returned to the mineralogy lab. He's been here ever since.

"I'm sorry the workload is overwhelming," I tell him.

"I'm not looking for sympathy." He taps the Sharpie against the clipboard. "I see this case is an expedite."

"My supervisor wants it closed yesterday. And . . ."

"What?"

"She's asking about agent transfers."

"Monday. I'll have something for you Monday. But you have to return the favor."

"No more blind dates with your friends."

He laughs. "I just want to hear about life as a special agent."

"That's it?"

"Start with what happened to your face."

We agree to meet back here for dinner tonight. Then I walk down the hall to Hairs and Fibers. Mike Rodriguez stands off the main gallery in a glass-fronted examination room holding a metal spatula. He scrapes down a pair of jeans that hang from a metal bar above white butcher paper.

"Wow, Raleigh." He shoves the safety glasses to his forehead. "Are you okay?"

"Fine. Really."

"That's some sunburn."

"Yeah, I'm fine."

"You're going to get ichthyderm."

Oh, the vocabulary of Hairs and Fibers. "And that would be . . ."

"Sunbather skin," he says. "Smoker's skin. The word translates literally from the Greek. *Ichthy* meaning fish, and *derm* meaning . . ."

After ten minutes, several Greek conjugations, and some scolding for using First-Aid tape instead of adhesive lifts, I manage to convey my urgent request to Rodriguez. He can't promise anything by Monday. I walk back to the mineralogy lab, but as I'm approaching the doorway, there's a faint, hollow clatter, like cheap spoons in a diner tossed into the cutlery bin. I watch Eric strap metal braces over his legs. When he glances up, his freckled face bears all the grief squeezing my heart.

"Sorry to tell you this," he says, "but no dancing to-night."

"Eric—"

"I got them in April. The wheelchair is next. I'll be out of the lab by September."

"What?"

"Can you see me, shuffling into a courtroom like this? The jury will take one look at me and slap 'handicapped' on the lab too. I'm a defense attorney's dream."

He continues buckling the braces, and I watch, feeling like I'm witnessing a slow-motion car crash. I want to make it stop, and I can't. It's beyond me. And it takes all my courage to ask the next question.

"Eric, can I pray for you?"

"Go right ahead," he says, working the braces. "I'm in no position to reject anyone's prayers. While you're at it, maybe you can get those holy rollers your mother hangs out with to pray for me too."

"I mean, now."

"Here?" He looks up. "In the lab?"

I nod.

"Raleigh." He smiles, placating me. "Listen, I appreciate your faith. Really, I do. It's gotten you through some tough times. But I don't believe that stuff. I'm a scientist. Big bang. The fossil record. *Evolution of the Species* is my bible."

"I know."

He glances past me to the examination areas, where his fellow esteemed scientists calculate precise figures about outcome and truth, everything based on fact. When his gray eyes return to mine, they are the color of ash. And full of doubt.

He nods. I close the door.

"Raleigh?"

"Yes?"

"Lock it."

16

Night falls over Richmond, suturing blue sapphire clouds to the city's amethyst sky. Broad Street tips its downtown fulcrum between light and dark as the pawnbrokers and ambulance-chasing lawyers close for the day, their alarms set, and the hookers and dealers stand in the growing shadows with palpable impatience.

But the Virginia Commonwealth University art building is wide open. And in the sculpture studio, white plaster coats Milky Lewis's black forearms.

"R-r-raleigh," he says. "What happened to your f-face?"

Whenever I hear Milky's stutter, I can't help wondering about the profound influence childhood wields over the rest of our lives. Medical experts might insist stutters are just weird physical glitches, random as birthmarks, but they would never convince me that Milky's speech impediment wasn't related to watching his mother sell herself across the Creighton Court housing project to stay high. Milky had six younger siblings, all from his mother's furtive unions. He fed the infants, toilet trained the toddlers, sent the young children to school. And when the time was right, he employed each of them as drug mules. His baby brother was shot dead during one delivery, and FBI agents were able to "persuade" Milky to talk. But even as he revealed himself, giving us names and numbers and locations, a mean and soiled regret clung to his dark eyes.

The eyes have changed slightly since then.

"You doing all right?" I ask.

"They put my sc-sc-sculpture out there."

"I saw the giraffe. Some joke about sticking your neck out?"

He pulls a lump of chalky plaster from a plastic bucket, massaging the wet clay between his large, dark hands. "I found some p-plastic tube. N-n-nothing to cut it with."

I want to warn him—don't tell the art snobs that last part. But it would be futile for several reasons. "Is this a good place to talk?" During dinner with Eric, Milky called my cell phone. I rushed back to Richmond, having waited all week for his call.

"I g-g-gotta lock the door."

He wipes his big hands on a dirty towel and leaves.

I stroll the studio. Dried white plaster sculptures stand on round wooden blocks, looming like half-formed ghosts. Much as I try, I can't decipher the body parts. But little here resembles reality. Helen and the art intellectuals find reality the basest aesthetic, a philosophy they bleed into their students. Standing in front of what might be an arm, I suddenly stop. My own reality is that I'm alone in a locked building with a convicted felon. At night. On instinct, I touch my

97

right hip, where my holster cradles a Glock. Unsnapping the holster, I run a quick mental rehearsal for the worst case.

When I turn around, Milky stands directly behind me, so close I can smell plaster dust on his skin. His dark eyes are flecked with yellow.

"I miss you, R-r-raleigh."

I take two steps back. "Helen says you're doing great."

He holds a six-inch putty knife—where did that come from?—and rolls the blade between his fingers. My mind flashes on Mike Rodriguez scraping down the jeans for evidence. "Milky," I start to say.

He does not hear me. His head bobs to some unheard rhythm, some deep bass line playing only in his mind. The rolling blade catches the overhead light, fracturing the spectrum into shards.

"Wuh-wuh-why can't I see you more?"

I step back. "Okay."

"N-n-nobody listens to me anymore."

The wooden base holding the sculpture bites my leg, pinning me in place. "Milky, remember what I told you?" He's still not listening. My right hand lands on the Glock, fingers curling. "Remember when you were surprised by the people in the Bureau? The agents. Remember how nice they were?" His brown eyes are glazed. "I told you people are generally nice, you just have to give them a chance. Remember?" I recognize this look. And when the knife goes up, I pull my gun.

But Milky's hand keeps going. He drops the knife, smothers his face with his palms. I watch him, my feet planted, both hands gripping the Glock.

98

"I'm st-st-stupid." He speaks into his arm. "St-stupid."

"If somebody called you stupid, Milky, they don't know you."

His sobs echo through the empty studio. The ghost statues watch, some grave chorus from a fallen world, a world that opened hours earlier when Eric Duncan strapped metal braces on his legs, when I saw the confused expression of a man intellectually certain all his life who suddenly can't say what tomorrow will bring. And now come the sobs of a powerful man who has done horrible things to equally horrible people, brought down by callow youth. The truth is, all the competencies we hold so dear eventually turn into our obstacles. Acute intelligence. Brute physical strength. Our sense of total self-sufficiency. They're illusions. At some point, we all feel naked and alone, and the longer we've relied on our competencies, the harder it is to surrender. I know; I'm like this. And when I see it clearly, I realize the old hymns got things right. *Broken, I came to thee, there is no other way.*

Still holding the Glock with one hand, I touch Milky's right arm, which is laid across his square face. The white plaster is drying like a cast over his dark skin. I listen to his ragged breathing slow down. He lowers his arm. He is not offended to see my gun. My experience with people like Milky is he'd be offended if I didn't pull my gun. We stand among the plaster ghosts, a hymn of silence running between us, broken only when sirens come screaming down Broad Street.

He asks me why I called, and I tell him the Bureau is

99

investigating the rooftop deaths at the Fielding factory. "Do you know anything about that?"

"Nasty." One of his favorite words. *Nasty* somehow never trips his tongue. He drops a haunch on the wooden stool, suddenly drained. "G-guy was weird."

"Hamal Holmes?"

"H-him and the cop."

"You knew them both?"

He shrugs, suggesting crime in Richmond is a quaint community of cops and robbers. And it is, that's why I called him. Tapping his temple with a plaster finger, he tells me Holmes wasn't right in the head. He bought crack from Milky's crew, first to drop weight for boxing, and later because he couldn't stop. Because nobody can stop. I wonder about the Coretta Scott King poisoning, whether the delusions were crack induced. After Hamal disappeared, Milky says he returned a new man.

"What about the detective?" I ask.

Milky crossed paths with Detective Falcon eight or nine years ago, he tells me. Falcon was a vice detective, and Milky was selling drugs. "I t-told you about that."

If I remember right, Milky served a year in juvie and never talked to authorities. It earned him wide stripes on the street.

"He wasn't n-nice like you."

"The detective?"

Milky describes an angry man, a cop who wouldn't budge, wouldn't compromise, wouldn't play nice.

"Given the circumstances," I tell him, "you probably didn't see his good side. Tell me more about Hamal."

"N-not right in the head."

"So you said. Can you be specific?"

For a while, nobody knew where Holmes went, he says. But when he came back to Richmond and took over the Second Street gym, there were no drugs. In fact, Holmes turned into a crusader for young black men, picking them off the street, keeping them off drugs, teaching them to fight. "B-but that place is nasty."

Since "nasty" describes a vast array of criminal activity, I ask, "What, exactly, is nasty about the gym, Milky?"

"You want s-s-something done, you go there."

"Something done," I repeat. "Something like . . . ?"

He picks up the putty knife, I lift the Glock. But the knife isn't for me. With one smooth motion, Milky draws the blade across his throat, a slow, simulated motion of death.

"You're telling me they killed people?"

He nods.

"You know this for a fact, Hamal Holmes killed people?"

Milky shrugs. "S-s-somebody in there took money for hits. Everybody knows it. Nasty b-business."

I tell him he's right: killing people is nasty business.

17

Outside the Richmond police department, near the flashing blue lights of a police cruiser, teenagers stand on the sidewalk, hollering at the cops. Inside the building at the reception desk wrapped in bulletproof Plexiglas, I show my identification. The guard buzzes the double doors, and I walk down the sulfuric yellow tile to the pebble glass door marked 102.

Detective Greene doesn't look surprised.

"You get those scratches hanging off the wall?" he asks.

"You heard about that."

"Big news around here." He takes one wooden chair and offers me the other. "Did you find anything? Oh, wait. I forgot. You get to ask all the questions."

"I didn't make the rules."

He leans back, evaluating. "You look . . ."

"Bad, I know. I got it already."

"I was going to say it changes my idea of an FBI agent."

"Maybe you have the wrong idea."

"I don't think so." He crosses his arms. "This civil rights case, totally bogus. But hanging off a roof by a rope? That takes some guts."

"Thanks." I mean it. "Did you find Detective Falcon's notes?"

He shakes his head.

"Two detectives," I say. "One room. Night work together. Long hours away from your families. You had to talk about your cases."

"I told you how we worked. Mike did his thing, I did mine."

"When Hamal Holmes quit breaking and entering, he bought into the boxing gym on Second Street. He kept his mother's bills paid. Made a gaggle of kids with his wife. DMV records say he drove a brand-new Lexus. The guy had money. And it wasn't from breaking and entering. And it wasn't from boxing."

"He threw Mike off that roof."

"The problem is that it makes no sense. Why would Holmes break into an abandoned factory? Even if he wanted to steal something, there's nothing in there. The dumbest defense attorney can prove he didn't break in. Then the widow Holmes can drive down here in her brand-new Bentley and spit on the precinct's steps."

His brown eyes compress. "Where you going with this?"

"I'm trying to put the pieces together, so this thing makes some sense. You told me your partner was dedicated to his work."

"He was a good cop," he says. "A great cop."

"Right. He didn't sit around collecting a paycheck."

He hesitates. "I told you, I don't know what Mike was doing up there."

"But it's a fair guess he was working a cold case that day. Maybe he got ticked off when he was assigned street patrol. He had real work to do."

"He didn't throw that kid off the building."

"But I think he was meeting with Holmes. Something went wrong."

"You're asking me to speculate again."

"You told me Detective Falcon went down to death row to interview that evil twin. V or T?"

"T. For Martin."

"So Martin the evil twin gives Detective Falcon some information, and it involves a cold case. Maybe the cold case involves Holmes."

The detective draws a deep breath. This time, I count seven beats. Eight. Nine.

And when he asks me to take a ride, I don't hesitate one second.

18

The grass at Chimbarazo Park is drought dry. The spindly elm trees are full of thirst. And the old Confederate hospital that once stood here is gone. In the aftermath of peace, the land has become headquarters for the city's battlefield parks. A small replica of the Statue of Liberty stands at the park's edge, donated by the Boy Scouts. Holding her tablet and her unlit torch, she looks over the dead grass with a gesture that seems both wonderful and terrible.

In his pristine Crown Victoria, Detective Greene reaches into the backseat, pulling a manila folder from a plastic bin, then silently reads the pages. The folder is not thick.

"Back in 1999, somebody up here called in a foul odor," he says. "Responding officers discovered two bodies at the edge of the park. Over there." He points out the windshield toward East Broad Street. "The recovered bodies were one male, one female. Teenagers. Male was never identified. Homicide ran dental records, fingerprints, whole nine yards. The kid didn't fit any missing persons reports. So John Doe kept his name."

"And the girl?" I ask.

"She turned out to be a prostitute. End of investigation."

"Wait—that's it?"

"No witnesses. No leads."

"So it's tossed in the cold case file."

He looks over at me. "I don't like it any more than you do."

I push back the questions, my mind flashing again on those file cabinets full of the unquiet dead. "Why are you telling me this?"

"This was Mike's ghost," he says.

"Ghost?"

"The case that haunts you. The one you want to solve more than any other, but it won't break. These two kids got dumped like garbage . . ." He looks over at me. "I don't know if I should tell you, but he and his wife, they had trouble making a family. I think that added to his obsession, because he kept saying, 'Somebody misses them.' He found the girl's people. But not the boy's; he was still looking." He reads me details. The girl was shot at the base of the skull, execution style. The bullets came from a .38, but no weapon was recovered. "She died instantly," he says.

"It's never instant."

He glances over. "You're probably right. But it was better than what the boy got." The medical examiner's report details the boy's punctured lungs, his teeth picked out of the dirt, a fractured skull. "Basically, he was beaten to death."

I stare out the windshield, trying to reconcile this

place, this city, this whole idea of two teenagers gone astray and left for dead on the same city block reserved for honoring the fallen in our unforgettable war. What did LuLu Mendant say? The wound is old, the wound is still open. Only the details have changed: Richmond remains a killing field. Around the park's perimeter, the fading Georgians and Victorians show big windows glowing with the cold blue light from television sets. Tonight the tired, the poor, the huddled masses yearning to breathe free—they're home watching reality TV.

"Were the bodies dumped here?" I ask.

"You're thinking somebody should have heard gunshots. But the boy's teeth were in the dirt, so he was beaten here."

"Nobody saw a thing."

He sighs. "We don't get a lot of cooperation. Your guy, LuLu Mendant lives right over there, on East Franklin. He controls the place."

"He's not *my guy*. He filed a complaint. We're pursuing."

The detective flips the file pages. I'm learning to wait through his pauses. When I glance at his visor, I see a prayer card wedged beneath the elastic band. A picture of Jesus—Jesus in the clouds, Jesus raising two fingers in blessing. A prayer for his dead partner.

"When Mike said T was ready to talk—"

"The twin, on death row?"

He nods. "He went because sometimes those guys want to unload, give up whatever's left of their conscience before they meet their maker. You don't agree with him, but that's why he went."

"The twins killed these two kids?"

"T swore they didn't do it."

"Maybe he was lying."

"Maybe."

"Did he tell him who did kill them?"

The detective turns to look out the windshield, and though I'm learning to wait through his pauses, he stares for so long that I finally turn to look, fully expecting to see something amazing, like the lighting of Liberty's torch. But there's nothing out there except this wide, dark street, this slice of city that's seen much brighter days. He hands me the cold case file and says, "I'm gonna need this back."

19

Saturday morning I wake with the jangly heartbeat of the overtired. There's only one way to get rid of it.

I lace up my running shoes and tiptoe across the courtyard. It's still too early for traffic on Monument Avenue, and the only sound comes from the birds greeting the dawn with *bob-white, bob-white*. I'm almost out of the courtyard when Madame spots me, her black nose pressed against the kitchen's French doors. Her tail wags as I reach in and grab her leash. Madame is not an animal who performs on a tether, but if we get caught breaking dog laws, I want backup.

We jog south down the Boulevard, where an armada of crepe myrtles prepare for floral fireworks. We turn into Byrd Park, jogging around the back lake where the cicadas hum like nervous woodwinds. Madame races from oak tree to poplar to ginkgo, culling canine clues from each trunk before leaving her own scent. But she never runs too far ahead, never falls too far behind. Every ten seconds or so, she turns her flap-eared head to find me, making sure all is well. She is one of the great dogs of a lifetime.

At the four-mile mark, I feel the day's heat coming on strong, so we cut over the RMA into the Fan. The neighborhood's tidy brick row houses lead us through Main Street, where the awnings advertise restaurants. Turning right on Grove Avenue, we slow to a walk near some scaffolding.

On the second story, DeMott Fielding scrapes paint from a windowpane. The plastic radio beside him plays that Allman Brothers song, the one about blue skies and sunny days, and for several long moments I stand on the sidewalk watching him work. The wait gets to Madame, and she barks.

DeMott looks down. "About time." He drops off the scaffolding with loose athleticism, brushing paint chips from his T-shirt. "That guy doesn't like me."

"Who?"

"The guy who took my note, at your house."

"Wally? He rents from my mother."

"Oh. I thought maybe he was your boyfriend. But that didn't make sense."

"Because he's black."

"No, because you wouldn't live with a guy before you were married. And he's not your type."

"What's my type?"

He opens his arms, grinning. "Someday you'll figure it out. Did you read my note?"

His note lies buried in my purse, covered by the stratigraphic record of every event following Nadine's breakdown on Wednesday. He's waiting for me to say something. Maybe his note's an apology for that night long ago, maybe it's an invitation to Mac's wedding. Either reason keeps me from reading it.

110

"Listen, I'm going over to Buddy's for breakfast," he says. "Come with me."

I look at the row house. It's in bad shape. "Don't you have work to do?"

"This house has been here ninety years. It's not going anywhere."

"Maybe another time." I start jogging, and Madame falls in beside me.

DeMott yells to our backs. "Call me, Raleigh!"

———

In the big house at the long pine table in the kitchen, Wally reads the *Richmond Times-Dispatch*. Under this table, you'll find my carved initials. And Helen's. And my father's and his sister Charlotte's, who later moved away, and several more generations of Harmon children who followed the tradition. I can't say how Helen felt, but I remember holding the butter knife and scraping through that soft yellow pine on the day David Harmon married my mother and adopted us as his children. Seeing my initials with all those other Harmons was like witnessing an official declaration, an act as solemn and official as a birth certificate.

This morning, my mother is standing at the stove, cooking something that looks like bacon and smells like bacon but I am absolutely certain is not bacon. Madame laps water from her bowl while I wash my face and hands in the sink. I inquire about breakfast.

"It's tempeh bacon!" she says.

Wally turns his head. "Fake-on. It makes a heart attack taste good."

111

Nadine wags the spatula at him. "Wally Marsh, I shudder to think about your health. If you ever ate something decent, your liver would collapse in shock." Her voice carries a happy lilt. She wears three-inch red slides with paisley pedal pushers. So no matter how bad tempeh bacon tastes, I will eat it. And if it keeps her good mood alive, I'll eat seconds.

After pouring a cup of coffee—"Shade-grown organic decaf," she informs me—I sit down at the table. Wally slides the paper's front section over, not making eye contact. I know something's coming.

The good news is "Fatal Rooftop Plunge" now runs below the fold. The bad news is the story still runs on A-1. The reporter, Carrie Bates, informs the city that an FBI agent "rock climbed" the factory. I *rappelled*, but never mind. And with that staccato writing style that makes everything sound both breathless and angry, the story quotes Victoria Phaup, who wants to remind everyone that the FBI is investigating every angle to the best of its ability; that the Bureau will not rest until the matter is completely resolved; that we take civil rights very seriously. Now I know she'll steam me for the rappelling episode, which I did not clear with her first.

And LuLu Mendant—never known to utter the phrase "no comment"—gets in his long two cents. "My people on Southside were victimized all over again," the mayor said. "The FBI dropped garbage on a peaceful protest. They threw trash on people." He claims Richmond police "physically abused innocent bystanders." And the reason the Bureau isn't making this "murder" a priority is because Hamal Holmes was black. "If he was a white man, they'd have ten agents out here every day."

Every endorphin from my run curls up and dies. I push the paper away.

Wally keeps reading. He only reads the features section, but he combs the town gossip column as if it's an illuminated manuscript from the Middle Ages.

"What's so intriguing?" I ask.

He looks up. "I can't figure this quote."

"Let's hear it."

"It's from a society lady—she won't give her name—but she's blabbing about another marriage falling apart." He glances over his shoulder. "Nadine, you know the Aikens?"

"Rosewell Aiken?"

"That's the one."

"Rosewell and Sannie Aiken?" she asks.

"Used to be."

"They were friends with your father," she tells me. "Rosewell works for that big law firm downtown." She sets the plate of tempeh bacon in front of me, along with whole wheat toast and what I'm betting is not butter. She puts a second plate on the floor for Madame, who sniffs the food carefully. Apparently, Wally is a nutritional lost cause.

"What kind of name is Sannie?" he wants to know.

"Sanford." Nadine rinses the frying pan in the sink. "Her mother's maiden name."

"That's Richmond," he says.

I break the fake bacon in half, it snaps like a dry twig. "What's the quote?"

"Rosewell left Sannie for another woman and—"

"Oh, dear," Nadine interrupts. "He'll never be happy now."

"I don't know," Wally says. "The other woman is a gorgeous young thing named Meade Ann Meeker. Meade—another maiden name gone amok."

But Nadine is no longer listening to him; she stares out the window facing General Lee and Traveller. "A foolish man devours all he has."

Wally looks at me.

"Proverbs," I tell him.

"She would haul the Bible into this."

She whips around. "I heard that, Wally. The Bible is the source of all wisdom. When you realize that, your life is going to take on real meaning."

"You saying my life doesn't have meaning?"

"I said *real* meaning. There's a difference."

"According to who?"

"According to the Bible, and if you would simply . . ."

I chew my food and let them hash out another evangelical version of "Who's on First?" The tempeh bacon is not bad, if you don't mind chewing, and the argument isn't all that terrible either. Back when Wally applied to rent the spare room here, I had some doubts. He seemed like a nice enough guy, raised by hardworking parents who sent their four children to Catholic schools. But Wally described himself as a "recovering Catholic." No ill will toward any faith, he told me, but those wooden rulers wielded by nuns beat the love of Jesus Christ right out of him. For that reason, he didn't seem a good match for my mother. But every other renter was worse.

There was the Wiccan and her candles. The computer geek who couldn't articulate one single sentence. And the girl who asked if her boyfriend could move in too. Wally's references checked out, along with my deep criminal background search. I even bribed Helen to ask around the VCU photography department, from which he graduated several years ago. The guy was universally admired. We signed a two-week test contract, during which I slept in a third-floor bedroom, wide awake every night. And every day Wally teased Nadine about everything from the way she dressed to her faith in God. Nadine acted upset, secretly loving the attention. Now, seven months into this arrangement, it was obvious my mother desperately needed something to do, and converting Wally to Christianity kept her very busy. More importantly, Wally dealt with her mental illness as though she suffered from nothing more than hiccups.

After washing down the tempeh bacon with organic decaf, I attempt to steer the conversation back on track. "So, what's the quote, Wally?"

Snapping the paper dramatically, he says, "I almost forgot. The woman says, 'Meade Ann is Rosewell's power mower.'" He lowers the paper. "All this time, I thought the brothers were coming up with the lingo. But here's some rich West End lady launching 'power mower.' That is good! Power mower!"

My mother shakes her head. "That's a Yankee for you."

"Meade Ann is a Yankee?"

"No, the quote, Wally. It's those Yankees, messing

things up again. A respectable Southern woman would never say the girl is Rosewell's power mower. That's ridiculous. She said she's his *paramour*. Those Yankees have tin ears. We should have won the war just for language alone." She looks at us. "Can't you hear it? Listen to me. Paramour, power mower. Paramour. Power mower. See?"

Wally glances at me. Nadine's right. And yet, we're both wondering the same thing, whether these words will hitch on her mind, compelling her to scrawl them forward, backward, sideways, scribbling until she breaks a code that doesn't exist.

"I like power mower better," Wally finally says.

I force my voice to sound casual. "Mom, you going to the camp today?"

She smiles. "Wally's coming with me!"

I raise an eyebrow.

"I'm just taking some pictures," he says defensively. "Don't get the idea this has anything to do with God."

"Nice pictures?" I ask.

"Raleigh, I don't take any other kind."

20

After a shower and change of clothes, I drive to McDonald's in Carytown, buying high-octane coffee and two Egg McMuffins, which I eat in the K-Car while listening to mostly static on my AM radio. Then I drive north on Interstate 95 to Ashland.

The Falcon home is located in King's Charter, a new subdivision that might sit on land originally granted by the king of England but today looks like most middle-class American neighborhoods: vinyl-sided homes lined up like dominoes, with street names like Tree Pond Drive, that have no trees, no ponds, and a lot of asphalt for driving.

When Janine Falcon answers the door, a blond toddler is riding her left hip. The boy's eyes are green as jade, like his mother's, but the rest of his face resembles his late father.

"May I help you?" she asks.

I introduce myself, showing my ID. Her pale face registers several emotions before finally going blank. She invites me into the living room, populated by oversized furniture upholstered in denim. The dining table holds bouquets of flowers in somber arrangements. Sitting on the sofa, she places the boy on the floor nearby.

"Did you know my husband?" she asks.

"No, ma'am."

She watches the boy navigate the living room, a Fisher-Price obstacle course.

"But he sounds like a devoted detective," I tell her.

Her green eyes stay on her son. "Mike hated working crowd control. I loved it. I always worried about him being a detective." She pauses, looking at me. "I can't understand why it happened this way."

After my father died, I came across a newspaper story about a meteorite that landed in upstate New York. The stone weighed 26 pounds and flew toward Earth at a speed approaching 33,000 miles an hour—roughly 4,000 times faster than the average cannonball and hurled by an asteroid belt between Mars and Jupiter that express-delivers tons of geologic material every year, though most of it lands in the oceans. But on this particular day, the meteor hit a car, killing the mother and child inside. The newspaper story quoted the husband, who kept asking, "Why?" It was the same question I asked after my father's murder.

"I'm sorry for your loss," I tell her. As usual, the words sound insufficient. Her face goes blank again. Here's another thing: after the meteor hits, your emotional reactions have the time delay of shell-shocked vets.

"M.J. keeps asking, 'Where's Daddy?'"

The boy turns his blond head. He stands at the other end of the room, near the dining table covered with the flowers. "Daddy?"

"No, honey." She smiles wanly. He returns to his toys. "I don't mean to be rude, but if you didn't know my husband, why are you here?"

"There's a civil rights case opened by the FBI—"

She stands up, her voice tight. "M.J., let's put in a video." The boy scrambles, chubby legs racing past the kitchen and down the hallway. He hollers, "Elmo! Elmo!"

She follows him, and I glance around the Falcon home. It's unusually bright, the way new houses are before daily life adds some character. The white fireplace mantel holds family photos. I see Michael Falcon, a heavyset man, probably once handsome. Another picture shows Mrs. Falcon holding the boy, both smiling wildly, their pale hair blowing in the wind. The boy wears a blaze-orange life preserver, obscuring everything but his face and arms.

"That was taken just a few weeks ago," she says as she walks back into the room. "We were out on the boat. Mike's dream was to fish for a living. Every man's dream, I guess."

"He must have been very proud of you two."

She nods. Her eyes are red. "He wanted to find a better job. Something nine to five so he could spend time with M.J. Now I keep thinking, what if . . ." Her voice trails off.

I went through those "what-ifs." What if David Harmon hadn't taken a walk that night. What if he hadn't always leapt to my mother's every whim. What if I hadn't moved to DC. Finally, I had to let them go. But I'm human. What-ifs creep back.

"Mrs. Falcon, do you know why your husband was on that roof Saturday?"

"He was doing his job." Her voice is almost shrill. "He was trying to protect people. Now my son will never know his father."

"I'm sorry about that."

"What am I supposed to do now?"

Her question echoes Mrs. Holmes, something I would never share with her. "Did your husband talk to you about his work?"

She shakes her head. "I didn't want to be part of it."

"He never talked about his cases?"

She gives me a hard look. "Are you trying to find out if he did something wrong?"

"I'm trying to find out what happened on that roof."

"Well, he didn't talk to me about work. But I know him better than anybody, and my husband would never, ever, do what these people are accusing him of. Never. Not in a million years would he throw a man to his death. That's sick."

I wait, giving her time to calm down. "Did he keep any work here?"

"There's an office," she says, "in the basement. He wanted to start a business, something he would run from home. That way he could spend time with M.J." Her lip trembles. "We just bought this house."

In the basement, next to the laundry room, Detective Michael Falcon set up a computer, printer, and fax, hanging certificates and commendations from the police department on the taupe-colored walls. A Virginia Tech Hokie, he hung his school's banner above the closet door.

"Mom-eee!" The boy.

She hesitates.

"Momm-eeeeeee!"

She looks at me. "Don't move anything. That's all I ask."

Inside the metal cabinet, hanging files are labeled for household bills, receipts, taxes, medical expenses. The Falcons filed joint tax returns. Mrs. Falcon left work last year, and payments are due on two cars. The boat is cleared. Two years ago, they received treatment at a fertility clinic. A file labeled "Horizon" outlines his plans for a private security firm.

Mrs. Falcon returns, brushing blond bangs over red-rimmed eyes. "I know my husband is innocent," she says. "He would tell me to cooperate with you."

"He really put some thought into that security firm." I hold up the file.

She nods. "He was only a year from early retirement. We decided he should stay with the department, because, you know, benefits and all." She pauses. "If I could do it over again . . ."

I ask to borrow some documents, promising to return them as soon as possible. She frowns. "I feel funny about that."

I offer my card, encouraging her to call the police chief and verify the investigation. Her doubt is subtle but palpable, like a soft breeze boding heavy rain. "You can call my supervisor as well."

"It's not that." She stares at my card. "It's just . . . you know?" Tears fill her emerald eyes.

I nod. I know. Beneath my bed, in one plain shoe box,

rests David Harmon's cheap Timex watch, the crystal smashed. In another larger box are some unfinished legal papers and notes, material I gathered from his desk the day after his murder. Most of those papers probably have no greater meaning. Last month, around Father's Day, I saw his Timex on sale at the local drugstore. But Janine Falcon's hesitation is the same irrational sentimentality that keeps me from throwing out that cheap watch. She wants to know—she needs to know—her husband once lived and breathed in the most mundane ways. Especially in mundane ways. It's the simple and ordinary that make people real, that can bring the dead back to life. These papers prove it.

She needs evidence.

And I need evidence too, for reasons that have nothing to do with bringing back the love.

21

Monday morning, Eric Duncan's mineralogy report hits my desk, faxed at dawn. I read it over and call the lab. He picks up on the fifth ring.

"I'm not too excited about green sand," I tell him.

"You're a geologist; it says glauconite."

"Yeah, glauconite. And some pyrite-bearing sediments in the clay. Whoopee."

"Did you read my notes about gray forms, dissemi-nated acid, clay? We're talking very fine sand, less than two microns."

One micron is about the thickness of a fingernail, equal to one one-thousandth of a millimeter. "It's good work," I say, "but green sand around this part of Virginia is like lobbyists in Washington—turn over a rock."

"The soil speaks, I don't speak for it." He sounds wounded.

"Sorry, I'm frustrated."

"I can hear it in your voice. Okay, look at the very end."

"Acrylamide, I saw that. Refresh my memory."

"Synthetic."

"Not ringing any bells."

"Dirt diamonds?"

"You mean that white stuff in potting soil?"

"Yep. Except this acrylamide didn't come from potting soil. And it didn't originate on the roof, it's not *in situ*." Acrylamide, he says, is used to manufacture plastics and in some water treatment facilities, where polyacrylamide polymers settle turbidity in drinking water. Also, paper plants use acrylamide to size their products. "And you might want to cut down on French fries because when certain starches are fried at high temperatures, they manufacture acrylamide, a known carcinogen."

"I doubt these guys were enjoying a Happy Meal."

He ignores me and says the brick and mortar samples are distinct, though not unique. "Distinct enough that I could match color and composition, if I had something to compare them to."

I tell him the shoes and clothes will make an express trip to the lab, once the police department releases the evidence. Then I thank him for the quick turnaround.

"Raleigh?" he asks.

"Yes."

He doesn't say anything else.

"Hello?"

"Somebody asked why we closed the door." His voice is muffled, as though his palm is cupping the receiver.

"What did you tell them?"

"I said you've lusted after me for years."

"That'll throw them off the trail."

He sighs. "I'm not as brave as you are. What I told

them was we had an important matter to discuss in private."

"We did."

"Yes," he agrees. "Yes, we did."

I wait. But it's more hollow silence.

"Anyway," he says. "Good luck with the case."

"I don't believe in luck."

"I know," he says. And hangs up.

22

The first synthetic rubies glittered to life about 200 years ago when a French chemist melted aluminum oxide at 2,200 degrees Celsius, tossed in some chromium, and voila—dazzling red gems and no need for a mining permit.

Within 100 years chemists had created synthetic emeralds, by cooking beryllium oxide in an alkaline solution at 800 degrees Celsius. Chemical gemology was off and running with only jewelers and geologists able to tell the difference. Nowadays, laboratories churn out thousands of synthetic gems from opals to diamonds, along with a host of minerals that don't occur in nature, such as my newest puzzler, acrylamide.

Science has come such a long way since those first rubies that it's even figured out how to produce babies in test tubes. And when I walk into the Richmond Reproductive Clinic, not one woman in the waiting room looks up from her magazine. The brawny, red-haired receptionist offers me an indulgent smile. "What time is your appointment, dear?"

I open my identification, discreetly laying it on the plastic counter. "I need to ask Dr. Chivigny some questions."

Painted eyebrows cinch her forehead. "What is this about?"

"I need to ask the doctor some questions," I repeat, using my Official Investigator voice so that I don't have to get rude and say, "No, you can't ask—just get the guy, will you?"

She exits through the side door; I turn around. Suddenly, every woman in the waiting room is staring at me, and the place feels too small for such fierce expressions. They are women with concerns, women with worries, women who have been denied the most basic right of being a woman: motherhood. They have come to a laboratory, when all around them other women receive the pure gems as though wishing were all it took. The last thing they want is a pall cast over their wild hope. I see it in their faces. *Questions? What kind of questions?*

Taking a seat near the exit, I stare at the blue Berber carpet. It is baby blue. The women return to their magazines, though occasionally I sense their glances. Finally, a short, bald man wearing a white lab coat appears, Dr. Chivigny. His name is embroidered above the chest pocket. Baby blue thread. "Please come back," he says.

I follow him down a narrow hall, past five doors with plastic bins holding medical charts. He closes his office door and shakes my hand. His fine-boned fingers explain his efficiency as a surgeon.

"I assume this is about the Spatz case," he says.

"Pardon?"

"Spatz, Harriet Spatz?"

I shake my head. Relief washes his narrow face.

"Oh, I thought . . ." He thinks a moment. "I have a case pending with a patient. A former patient."

"I'm with the FBI."

"Yes, I know, my receptionist told me. But I assumed since it's national now—the Spatz woman alleges a drug she took under my care deformed her baby. It's not possible, of course. Several clinical studies prove Lupron does not cause birth defects. But facts don't matter to personal injury lawyers, and they've launched a national search for women who took Lupron." He takes a breath. "Never mind. What can I help you with?"

"I'm not here to investigate you. I wanted to ask about a couple who used your clinic. Michael and Janine Falcon."

"Falcon, Falcon. The name doesn't have any immediate association. Please, make yourself comfortable. I'll be right back."

His desk is one thick slab of a tree trunk, shellacked to show hundreds of tree rings. I start to wonder whether the doctor is capable of metaphor, with all the baby blue references and a table that insinuates his ability to extend family trees. When he comes back, I decide not.

"Michael and Janine Falcon, yes, patients of mine." He carries their file. "You'll have to excuse me. I don't get to know my patients well."

"Seems like you would."

"This appears to be an intimate scenario, doesn't it? But once a woman conceives, I am no longer her physician. She returns to her regular ob-gyn for the remainder of the pregnancy. The less I know about them, the better." He catches himself. "For them, of course."

128

"Of course."

"So let's see . . ." He flips through the medical file. "The Falcons were under my care for thirteen months. She conceived on the third IVF . . ."

The doctor is under investigation; he is eager to help if it will gain my goodwill and alleviate some of his trouble. I'm not about to set him straight. Not when Janine Falcon won't release this particular file.

"IVF?" I ask.

"In vitro fertilization," he explains.

"That's a complicated procedure."

He almost shrugs. Except that gesture would undermine his prowess. "I perform about a dozen every week. After harvesting the eggs, I implant them in the woman's uterus. Then we wait. What was your name again?"

I give him my card.

He holds it carefully; he might need it later. "Miss?"

"Yes."

"Miss Harmon, if this doesn't have to do with the Spatz woman, may I ask what these questions are about?"

I tell him Michael Falcon is dead. For one split second, the doctor grimaces. He asks what happened, so I explain that Mr. Falcon was a Richmond detective who died last week falling from a Southside roof.

He nods. "I heard about that on the news. But I didn't pay attention to the details. I honestly do not remember him. Most husbands never set foot in my office. Embarrassment, shame, challenged manhood, a whole gamut of reasons. Still, I don't see my connection to your investigation."

And he doesn't need to. I keep going. "How much does this IVF procedure cost?"

"Making a baby is an expensive enterprise, and most insurance plans do not cover infertility treatments. I offer qualified patients the option of making monthly payments. It cuts down on their paperwork. When the bank gets involved, it can be too much for couples to handle."

I ask about cost again, trying to pin him down.

"One IVF treatment costs about fifteen thousand dollars."

"If Mrs. Falcon underwent three treatments, that's about, what, forty-five thousand dollars?"

He thumbs through the medical file. "I also performed some diagnostics and six in-utero inseminations."

I wait for explanations.

"People call it the turkey-baster method. Of course, it's not that simplistic."

When I wonder aloud about the Falcons' monthly payments, he flips through the file. "More than a thousand dollars per month."

I'm shocked, and it shows.

He smiles. "That's not unusual," he says. "One family paid me more than one hundred thousand dollars to conceive one child."

"Cheaper to adopt."

"You don't have children, do you?"

I shake my head.

"May I ask, how old are you?"

Twenty-nine, I tell him. He nods. "My patients are mostly professional women who have put off having a family. After age thirty, a woman's fertility drops precipitously. Heroic measures are necessary. My success rate is about 45 percent."

Is he really advertising his services? Then he won't like my response. "So more than half your patients don't conceive."

His smile tightens. "The chance they might offers them great hope."

"Enough hope to go deep into debt."

"Correct. But it's a tremendous comfort to the widow," he adds.

"Having the child."

"Well, that, certainly. But the Falcons' bill is paid in full." He turns the folder so I can read the balance page, where the two-inch red stamp marks the account closed.

When the doctor asks if there is anything else, I thank him for his time. He's been generous with information, so generous we now have a tacit understanding of back-scratching: I might not be able to help with the Spatz problem, but I won't report him for breaking privacy laws.

As I'm leaving, he says, "Miss Harmon, don't take this the wrong way, but I hope we don't meet again. For your sake, and mine."

23

The James River plantations roll toward the water on my right. Under the canopy of ancient trees, Route 5 feels like a ribbon leading to that bygone era of wealth and oppression, heroism and tragedy. And I wonder whether living in such a hallowed atmosphere is what causes the Fieldings to behave as they do, as though rules don't apply to them.

When the leafy canopy parts and the sun hits the K-Car hood, the spell is broken. And the mighty James makes its way to the sea, bearing sediment and history with equal indifference.

On the last stretch of Route 5, I wind through Williamsburg and park behind the colonial village compound. From the K-Car's backseat, I pull out a wide straw hat. The backseat looks like I go on auditions for a living because there's an extra set of clothing for every conceivable circumstance. Too many times I've been pulled for duty with no chance to get home and change clothes. My camera is back there too, along with geology equipment and gym stuff that rarely gets used.

I merge with the tourists shuffling down Duke of

Gloucester Street, filing past the colonial taverns and wooden stocks sanitized to theme-park standards. Behind me, a small boy blows a tin whistle, the kind kiosks sell from the oyster-shell roads. I cross the street to the College of William and Mary campus, heading for the geology department.

During summer breaks from Mt. Holyoke College, I took a job with the Virginia Department of Mining and Mineral Resources. The state keeps plenty of records on mountains, valleys, lakes, rivers, and streams, but what lies beneath those surfaces is almost unknown. And with subdivisions like King's Charter devouring the terrain, the state decided to hire budding geologists like myself to hike across the Old Dominion mapping the soil. It was during my second summer that Richard Burke crossed land in Petersburg belonging to dirt farmers. The fields were full of black sand, which the farmers had cursed since the Civil War. That black sand was biotite, a prized manufacturing mineral. Sure enough, the day after Richard announced his discovery in a geology journal, mining company reps descended and the dirt farmers won Nature's lottery: suddenly they were millionaires.

Behind the college's annex, I find Richard's part-time office. Now that the mapping is over, he is teaching courses at William and Mary two days a week. His office is armed with olive drab map cases and books stretching to the ceiling like stalagmites. We spend ten minutes catching up on rock hunts before we get to the reason for my visit.

"When we were mapping the state, you swore us to

confidentiality." Mining reps start asking questions, hoping you'll slip and say you just found aluminum ore outside Abingdon.

He stares through thick glasses, stroking his white beard. "Why do you ask?"

"I need that same promise from you now."

"Does this involve a criminal case?"

"Yes."

"You have my word."

The minerals Eric found in the roof soil—glauconite, pyrite, acrylamide—are all I can give him. If this case ever goes to court, some defense attorney can allege an outside soil scientist knew too much, compromising the evidence.

Richard walks over to the map cases, yanking open several shallow drawers. Thirty minutes later, we've covered his office with maps from the U.S. Geologic Survey, including a cross-sectional analysis of Virginia's Coastal Plain—Richard's specialty.

To explain Virginia's geology, the cartographer needs every color in the palette. Ancient molten lava is covered by marine sediment deposited by glaciers that eroded the mountains that were produced by an earthquake that ran along a fault line. Virginia's map is so aesthetically beautiful that if I removed all the scientific explanations, my sister, Helen, would demand to know who this brilliant abstract artist was—then turn apoplectic when I told her, "God."

Eight formations near Richmond are capable of producing the green sand in the roof sediment. Eight is far too many. Like I told Eric, glauconite is too plentiful to be helpful. But pyrite—otherwise known as fool's gold—narrows the search considerably.

"Pyrite sands with glauconite is an unusual combination," Richard says, "especially here in the Coastal Plain. Would it compromise the case if I knew where the soil sample came from?"

"I can tell you it was an urban setting."

"Construction site?"

I shake my head.

From one of the stalagmites, he pulls out a geochemistry textbook, offering a mini-primer on acids and acylides. "If you drive along Interstate 295, you'll see some gray-green soil on the roadside. But you won't see any grass or flowers, and the concrete barriers are crumbling. That's because the acid in that soil kills anything. The soil literally eats through concrete, even steel rebar."

"You're saying this soil is exposed next to the highway?" Anybody could carry that on the bottom of their shoe. Any cop pulling over a speeder.

"Don't look worried," he says. "It's above the road. Nobody's walking through that stuff, except the guys replacing the concrete every three years. But that's not the only occurrence. I always tell my students—"

"Think of the earth as a layer cake." I finish his sentence.

He chuckles. "I'm an old broken record."

"You're a good teacher."

"Thank you," he says. "So we have our layer cake. Deep down in the cake is the glauconite and pyrite. Lower Tertiary deposits. But to expose them on the surface, you have to slice the cake. Building a highway is one knife."

He traces his finger over the map, pointing to two other places where the cartographer swirled mustard with pine green ribbon to show the occurrence of pyrite and glauconite. The first spot is northwest of Richmond, next to the South Anna River. The second is east of Richmond, beside the James River.

"The other method is to have water cut the surface," he says. "The rivers reveal those lower layers."

"Still, anybody could pick up this stuff on their shoe," I tell him. "And it's more than one location."

"Yes, but you mentioned acrylamide."

"That one threw me."

"Don't feel bad. Synthetics throw me too."

But some years ago, an industrial company wanted to build a production facility just north of Richmond. The state commissioned an environmental impact study, and Richard did the work. "Paper manufacturer."

"They use acrylamide to size paper."

He grins. "You did some homework. Good." The company got approval to build the paper plant, despite acrylamide leaching into the soil. "The area's so full of acidic pyrite, nothing grows there anyway." He points to the South Anna River, where water cuts the Earth's cake, serving up glauconite and pyrite, garnished with acrylamide. "Right there."

"No acrylamide anywhere else?" I ask.

He shakes his head. "And I'm your expert witness."

24

When I get to the office that afternoon, the place has cleared out. On the horizon, a laurel of graphite clouds is waiting for the signal to advance—another thunderstorm. Everyone rushes through the parking lot, rolling up car windows or leaving early for home.

But Phaup is here. And she immediately calls me into her office.

I give her the lab results, then explain how the roof soil occurs in only two places around Richmond. Soil so distinct that if we find it in both men's shoes, we will know for certain they met before colliding on the roof. "But I need the victims' shoes to proceed, and Internal Affairs won't share the material evidence."

She picks up a yellow pencil tattooed with chew marks. "Raleigh, this is a civil rights case. We will never know what happened on that roof."

"I'm close to finding out."

"Every agent feels that way. But that's a subjective evaluation. I've already told you, I want this case closed immediately."

"But the U.S. Attorney's office can subpoena the police for the shoes and clothes."

"Yes," she says, "we need to call the attorney's office."

I stand, eager to do just that, when she adds: "Only ask for a declination."

"Declination?" I sit down.

"Yes. We decline further investigation and prosecution of this case," she says, as though I'm asking for the term's definition. "We have no witnesses, physical evidence is sketchy, and no way we can prosecute."

"But the evidence isn't sketchy. It's just withheld."

"Consider this a rite of passage, Raleigh. Ninety-nine percent of all our civil rights investigations wind up like this—"

"But that 1 percent—"

"If this case were that 1 percent, I would not assign a junior agent."

I let the insult pass. "I have reason to believe the detective was meeting Holmes on the roof that day. I can prove it."

"The dirt, right. Good call there. And I expect you to use that forensics tool again," she says sarcastically, ordering me to call the attorney's office for the declination.

Then I'm excused.

———

Rain comes later that night, a good soaking storm that pounds the carriage house's metal roof, sending rivulets of tears down my windows.

But Richmond's summer rains are Napoleonic, mostly short and furious, and during the storm's final rumbles,

I pull on a baseball cap and drive down Monument Avenue past the statue of J. E. B. Stuart atop his rearing horse.

During my senior year at Mt. Holyoke, I taught the lab portion of Introductory Geology, a course nicknamed nationwide Rocks for Jocks. Among my science-challenged students was a girl named May-Ling Lee. She was also from Richmond, and later took a job with the *Richmond Times-Dispatch* writing obits—in fact, she wrote my father's obituary. With good grace, she attended his funeral, endearing herself to me forever by slipping a piece of staurolite into my hand. In the far reaches of southwest Virginia, staurolite is popular for country baptisms because its pale crystals twin at right angles, creating perfect white crosses. Plenty of chemical theorems can explain how this happens, but Virginia's mountain people claim the rocks fall directly from heaven, from the angels who cried over the death of Christ.

Last year, the Richmond newspaper promoted May-Ling from obits to the night cop beat. Periodically, she now calls me with law enforcement questions, which are answered as deep background, never attributed. Tonight, I find her sitting at her desk in the newsroom. And her desk looks oddly familiar—an authentic fire hazard with stacks of notebooks, police manuals, paper coffee cups, and press releases. When she smiles at me, she reveals a slight overbite that gives her a guileless expression. Which I'm sure helps in her line of work.

"Got a few minutes?" I ask.

Outside, the street sends up that peculiar aroma of hot

wet concrete, the smell of summer swimming pools. We walk down to the Fourth Street Diner and take a secluded table on the second floor, May-Ling setting the police scanner next to the ketchup bottle, adjusting the radio's volume so the crackle can be heard above the jukebox. The waitress plunks two glasses of Coca-Cola on the blue Formica. When May politely asks for a straw, the waitress throws a withering look, stomps downstairs, stomps back up, and throws the straw on the table, slapping down the tab before leaving again.

"Crabbiest waitresses in town." She sips. "So what brings you here at midnight?"

I explain our civil rights investigation, that I'm looking into the rooftop deaths.

"That was you, wasn't it? On the building?" She laughs. "I knew it!"

"On your cop beat, did you ever meet Detective Falcon?"

"Raleigh . . ." She stabs her straw into crushed ice.

"My turn to ask the questions. Deep background, off the record, whatever terms you use with me."

"You swear on Mary Lyon's grave?"

"I swear on Mary Lyon's grave." This is the other part of our deal: we invoke the name of Mt. Holyoke's founder. For alums her name is like "Semper Fi" for Marines.

May glances out the diner's window, the plate glass layered with so much grease the traffic light at Fourth and Main is a smear of primary colors. "People speculated Falcon was dirty."

"Dirty. In what way?"

"On the take," she says.

140

"Where'd that come from?"

"He had a new house in Hanover County. New boat, new baby. But it was common knowledge he planned on taking early retirement. Cops don't make that kind of money, and cops with those expenses don't cut out early."

The only item Janine Falcon let me borrow was the file on her husband's security firm, which budgeted $150,000 for the first year. "Maybe he was going into another profession."

She shrugs. "They were good sources, Raleigh. But now, forget it. Nobody will ever say anything bad about the guy again."

"Did you ever meet him?"

"I wrote a story about him." Her jaw drops. "You don't read my stories?"

"Nothing personal, the newspaper gives me heartburn."

"My story was about the cold case unit with Detective Greene. Hard guys to interview," she says. "Like talking to a wall. But they have an incredible clearance rate. They solve 80 percent of what they open."

"Maybe the accusations against him were professional jealousy."

"Cops go bad, even good detectives," she says. "I can't really blame them. They make no money, druggies want to kill them, and when they screw up one little thing, reporters like me swoop in and write about it."

"You almost sound sorry."

"I'm not," she says. "I'm not sorry about the stories. The press keeps the cops honest. But I see how they'd get tempted." She glances at her watch, picks up the scanner. I lay two dollars on the table, and we walk outside. At midnight, the humid air feels soft as sea foam.

"What was your opinion of him?" I ask.

"Your basic veteran cop."

"And what's that?"

"Tired. Wary of reporters. Angry."

"Dirty?"

"I'll never know," she says. "And now the guy's a dead hero."

25

In the morning, I drive my mother to the Pentecostal camp while Madame keeps her nose out the Benz's window. Worship service is sparse, with a wiry man on the stage. His large family stands with him. My mother moves toward the electric organ, swaying with the melody. Fifteen minutes later, nothing's changed, and I jog across the campground to the car. When I open the door, Madame jumps in.

"No, girl," I tell her. "You have to stay."

She doesn't move.

"C'mon, Madame. Out."

She places her paw on the gearshift. This dog's unbelievable.

"All right, but you have to stay close. You hear?"

She leaps to the passenger side, and we head north on Route 1, turning right five miles later, driving directly east into the morning sun. Two miles later, I pass the Bull Island Paper Plant and a narrow overpass. I park on the soft shoulder.

The South Anna is an ancient waterway riddled with oxbows, moving sideways as much as forward. Near its riverbanks the kudzu vines climb gum trees, reaching over the muddy water like leafy bridges leading nowhere. Madame follows me down the concrete boat ramp. Sure enough, it's crumbling. I take out a film canister to collect the colluvium of rock fragments and soil. To the side of the ramp, I fill another canister, where trailer wheels have cut creases into the soil.

I fill three more canisters, at the water's edge, rubbing the soil between my fingers. Like wet clay, it feels creamy, sensuous. Taking off my tennis shoes, I wade into the water and plunge more canisters to the river bottom, scraping for samples. I wait for Madame to finish her own investigation, then we walk back to the car. A blue Chevy truck hauling an aluminum fishing boat passes us on the road. I watch the driver pull a four-point U-turn across the narrow two-lane road. He leans out his window, fishing lures dangling from his faded green hat.

"How ya doin'?" he asks.

"Nice spot you got here."

"Don't I know it."

"Does it get busy?"

He shakes his head. "Not too many know about this place. Kind of a secret. Like to keep it that way, know what I'm saying?"

"Yes, sir."

He nods, touching his hat before backing the boat down the ramp, exactly the way I imagine Detective Falcon used to do.

———

Nadine says it's too hot to dance. Last night's rain saturated the air with humidity. We leave the camp early. I get to the office around one o'clock, slipping into my cattle stall and dialing the mineralogy lab in Washington. I tell Eric to expect some soil comparison samples via Bureau mail, then ask him to transfer me to Hairs and Fibers.

"Didn't I send you that report?" Mike Rodriguez says.

"No, Mike, you didn't."

Five minutes later, a hairs and fibers report arrives by fax. I snap up the pages and scurry back to my desk. As I read the report, a giant stopwatch ticks inside my head. The strand of hair lifted from the brick belonged to a black male. Soft tissue from the scalp was attached to the follicle, so the hair can provide a DNA profile—further instructions needed. The blue fibers are nylon; the red fibers are leather, heavily treated.

I quickly type up a request for Rodriguez to run a nuclear DNA profile on the hair. Then I pick up the phone.

Somebody stands to my right, where my stall opens into the B Squad cattle yard. Phaup.

"Raleigh, do you have that declination?"

I wave the phone. "Calling the attorney's office right this minute, ma'am."

She walks away, adjusting her undergarments, and I dial the U.S. Attorney's office downtown, asking for Charles Reynolds. I tell him we're looking into possible civil rights violations that might have occurred on the roof of the Fielding hat factory.

He grunts. "How's that going?"

I tell him we have soil from the roof, very specific soil, as distinct as a fingerprint. The lab's Hairs and Fibers unit can get a DNA profile from one hair collected from the factory's brick. "But I don't have any witnesses. And Richmond PD won't release the victims' shoes and clothes. Internal Affairs claims it's a pending investigation."

"You want a subpoena?" he asks.

I'm fairly certain most of my trouble comes from sins of omission rather than commission. I tend to withhold vital information rather than lying outright, such as telling my mother I'm only a geologist. Omission means you can still convince yourself it's not a lie. And now I'm going to do it again. "What would you say about a declination?" I ask.

His voice barrels through the phone line. "What?"

"Don't you think a declination would be the best thing," I continue, my conscience waging a losing war, "since there's not enough evidence here to prosecute?"

His voice fills with the lyrical emphasis of Southern blacks, a righteous tone full of inflection. "Let me explain something to you, Raleigh. I grew up on Southside. I know these people, I *belong* to these people. And if you guys blow past this one, we're gonna lose whatever *frac*tion of credibility we *enjoyed* with that community. Forget about any future *cooperation* from these folks. Our goose'll be cooked for good."

"But I've got no witnesses. Six hundred people out there, and nobody saw a thing."

"These two guys took a dive—what—last week?" he says. "And already you're asking for a declination? What's the matter with you, girl?"

146

Pride wants to save face, tell Charlie the declination wasn't my idea. It's Phaup's idea. But I hang on to one last shred of integrity while he continues lambasting me.

"You're not going to get witnesses. Not honest ones. That's how it works on Southside. Know why? Because the Feds do stupid things like ask for declinations one week into a civil rights investigation."

I wait quietly, wondering if my chastisement is over. No.

"You should've called me right away when the cops pulled this stunt with the evidence. I'll have a subpoena ready this afternoon."

"You're sure about this?"

"The case stays open, Raleigh. No declination."

————

In her office Phaup is reading some green sheet reports, which means some poor agent is going to have to account for every single routine procedure. I knock on the door. She motions me in.

"I just called the attorney's office."

"Good." She points to a leather club chair opposite her desk. "I realize this is difficult, Raleigh. As an agent you're trained to pursue every case to its conclusion. But with more experience you'll understand why we closed this one."

I open my mouth; she cuts me off.

"Civil rights is a hornet's nest," she continues. "We go in and get stung all over." She smiles, enjoying her metaphor. Her desk drawer is probably full of them.

147

"There's never any meaningful resolutions. I'm simply sparing you the frustration."

"Yes, ma'am."

"Every agent learns to let go of certain cases. And now, we can move on."

"We could, if the attorneys gave us the declination."

Her dark eyes narrow. "What's that?"

"They refused to grant a declination."

"Refused," she repeats. "You told them we're *asking* for the declination?"

"Yes, ma'am."

"We are *requesting* the declination?"

"Yes, ma'am."

"And they *refused*."

I nod. "They want us to subpoena Richmond PD for the physical evidence."

She tries to read my face, but I'm granite right now. One false move . . . She swivels her enormous office chair so that it faces Parham Road, and I'm left staring at the chair's wide back for several long moments. When finally she turns around again, her voice sounds as flat as a delta. "With whom did you speak?"

"Charles Reynolds."

She punches the phone, telling her secretary, Claudia, to dial the U.S. Attorney's office downtown. Phaup gets transferred twice, and when Charlie's supervisor picks up, she lifts the receiver, severing the speakerphone. I can hear her explain the case is not coming together. No witnesses, we defer to the police investigation, we have manpower needs in other areas. She does not tell him civil rights is a waste of time.

When she hangs up, she looks at me levelly. "Con-gratulations."

I will myself not to move, not so much as blink.

"Understand my words, Raleigh. If I'm forced to say this again, there will be dramatic consequences."

I press my forearms into the chair, holding my breath.

"You get what we need to resolve this case. Nothing more. Are we clear?"

I nod.

She swivels back to the window. I stand to leave.

"Raleigh?"

"Yes, ma'am."

"I expect this to be finished very soon. Will that be a problem for you?"

"No problem," I tell the chair.

26

At 5:46 p.m. Charlie Reynolds walks from the federal courthouse to the Richmond police department, bearing a subpoena for Harrold Teddrow, supervisory head of evidence. In the sulfur-tiled lobby, I watch Charlie shrug into a seersucker jacket. Sweat beads his forehead, glistening against his nearly obsidian skin.

"How come you don't sweat?" He wipes his brow with a handkerchief so heavily starched it barely absorbs perspiration.

"I sweat."

"Not what I've seen," he grumbles.

We find Harrold Teddrow outside the evidence room, and Charlie hands him the subpoena. Teddrow holds it with both hands, his blue uniform puckering at the buttons, sagging at the shoulders, as though it was once evidence released into his possession. He scratches stubble on his chin.

"It's all legit, Teddie," Charlie tells him.

"I figure it is. I'm just wondering who's gonna get ticked off more, the chief or Owler in IA." He sighs. "I don't want to deal with either of them. It's late. I want to go home." He looks at Charlie, lowering his voice. "Besides, nobody likes that ferret in IA."

With a ring of keys, Teddrow unlocks the steel door protecting the evidence room. The place looks like a communal garage for the deranged—a prosthetic leg ends mid-thigh, propped next to a stained-glass window with two bullet holes, blood spatters a white bearskin rug, and three mangled fenders stand with an electric amplifier and four shovels bagged with plastic. With another key, Teddrow opens a yellow locker and pulls down two plastic bags. He hands one to Charlie, one to me. The bags are heavy, bulky.

"Thanks, Teddie," Charlie says.

"You got the papers, you get the goods."

"I mean, thanks for not making waves."

Teddrow shrugs, the uniform creeping across his shoulders. He slams the locker shut. "No need to make waves. They find out what just happened, it's gonna be tsunami city around here."

———

I drop Charlie at the federal courts building, promising to come to his church in New Kent soon. Then I drive to the office, feeling both anticipatory excitement and dread.

Years from now, the personal effects of dead people might not bother me so much. All my work in the lab was fairly detached—except for items like Ellie Mullins's lungs, because an agent combed through the evidence first, sending only what mineralogy needed to see. But outside our evidence collection room, I hold a three-

151

inch gold crucifix and see the face of Bernadette Holmes weeping in her kitchen. I hear the children yelling in the back room. I see the widow, deeply wounded. Hamal Holmes's clothing is stiff with blood and human tissue lodged into the folds of his faded blue jeans. His wallet holds nothing significant. No wedding ring is found, so I heat-seal the crucifix and the wallet into a plastic bag and drop them into the vault.

Detective Falcon died in Dockers and a sport shirt. Both stiff as boards now. His wallet holds pictures of his wife and son, and I heat-seal it with his gold wedding band and a watch, smashed, hands frozen at 12:07. I note the time in my notebook, wondering whether Janine Falcon will keep this watch the way I have, to mark the time when time stopped.

I stare at the two pairs of shoes.

Hamal Holmes's are made by Nike, red and black suede. The soles consist of narrow swirls of amber rubber. I brush a gloved finger over the suede, trying to decide whether the fibers on the wall could have come from these shoes. With tweezers, I scrape soil lodged in the treads and place it in a marked film canister.

The detective's shoes are brown leather, lug-soled, the deep crevices packed with soil. It drops easily into another canister, and I sign an evidence log with my name, case number, and time, then press the buzzer on the wall.

Allene Carron opens the Dutch-door window. The woman is as nice as they come, but after working her way up from FBI clerk to head of evidence control, after witnessing fifteen years of paperwork, she is legitimately

152

skeptical of any agent's ability to correctly fill out forms. Allene rereads my documents for errors, finds two, then assigns the evidence a barcode, scanning it into the Bureau's database.

"Today's your lucky day," she says. "The last mail leaves in fifteen minutes, so this'll get to DC tonight."

———

Upstairs at my desk, I phone Eric's voice mail, explaining that evidence is on its way. I remind him that the case needs to be resolved very soon or I'm on my way to Sioux City. I leave Rodriguez a message too, asking for DNA on the hair and for comparisons with the fibers from the shoes and clothing I'm sending tonight.

Then I pack up and drive to the James River.

27

On summer evenings, flame-hued fog rises from the James River, ghostly with the sunset, a watery shroud whispering of the devastation and loss, the ripples of conflict echoing through the ages and still felt today.

It's nearly eight o'clock when I pull into an unnamed park off Route 5 after stopping by the house to tell Wally to watch Nadine tonight. The geology map on the bench seat says this is the only other place glauconite and pyrite are exposed at the surface, and the park has a boat ramp. Also crumbling.

But this time, my walk down the ramp is awkward. I'm wearing Wally's hip waders, and the rubber boots make me wide in the middle, narrow at the feet, like a very fat woman wearing teeny-tiny shoes. No grass grows near the boat ramp. In fact, not much grows anywhere in this no-name park, just some spindly pines circling the parking lot, dropping sharp orange needles on already acidic ground. At the bottom of the ramp, I fill two film canisters then head west along the river's marshy bank. The evening sun dips behind Richmond's skyline while mud grabs my feet like desperate hands. I yank my legs out, moving against the current.

While the map tells me pyrite and glauconite are here, I need to find some acrylamide to complete the soil profile. Along the South Anna, the easy deduction was the paper plant. But out here, I can't say where acrylamide would come from. Farther ahead, a nest of Styrofoam cups and paper trash swirls alongside of the river. I pull a plastic bag from my pocket and deposit torn coffee cups, soggy fast food wrappers, and one waterlogged magazine with pictures of naked girls whose facial expressions suggest they prematurely donated their brains to science.

Across the water, two smokestacks rise against the dimming sky, a red light bleating on each. It's an old sawmill, the one that used to make Southside smell like rotten eggs. Like so many of the mills over there, it closed some years ago. But maybe acrylamide was used there; maybe the synthetic mineral sifted into the soil downriver. I glance back up at the sky and see the first stars winking into appearance, sparkling against the sapphire background. If I hurry, I can drive over the bridge and take samples by the sawmill. I turn and walk to the boat ramp, but my feet slip in the muck. And it's difficult to see where I'm going. I kick myself for leaving my flashlight in the car, for being in such a hurry to get this done. For stability I wade closer to shore, feeling the river's current push me from behind. I look up, searching for the boat ramp.

Cigarette. The ember smolders red. Then disappears into the dark. I slow down, considering scenarios.

155

A voice says, "How ya doin', honey?"

I tug my feet from the mud.

"Kinda late to be fishin'," he says.

Two men. No shirt on one. Sleeveless undershirt on the other. I smell something sour. Not cigarette smoke.

"You need some help?" he asks.

I'm standing at the bottom of the boat ramp, my boots weighted with mud. In my hands, I hold the plastic bags of trash and the canisters of soil. My flashlight is in the car. Along with my gun. My heart skips a beat.

"You ain't from around here," he says.

The second man holds a tree branch thick as a baseball bat. With the tip, he traces the water. I buy time, kicking my boots against the boat ramp, knocking muck off the bottoms, the concrete crumbling at my touch. When I step on the ramp, the first man moves to the side. His hair is shaved, nearly bald. The second, with the stick, falls behind. His skin is the color of wheat chaff.

"What'd you say your name was?" the first one asks.

The gravel path leading to the parking lot, to my car, to my wonderful car, is thirty yards away.

"Well, let me introduce myself. My name's Oscar."

I keep walking, the waders undulating around me, making rubber *waw-waw* sounds. I want to run, sprint full speed, but the boots are forcing me into mincing steps.

"Oscar," he says again. "Oscar Weiner."

Their laughter gets boxed in by the dark, by the narrow pines and the indifferent water flowing behind us. I keep my eyes on the K-Car, its back wheels against a log boom, front facing out. I'm suddenly grateful for my habit of always backing in, grateful for one small precaution when I forgot so many others. My cell phone is in my bag, on the passenger seat. *You were rushing.*

"Hey, lady." The second guy. "Didn't you hear Oscar?"

I tuck the plastic bags under my left arm and reach into the waders with my right hand, searching for my car keys. He grabs my arm, whipping me around. The keys fly out of my hand. I hear them land with a metallic flutter somewhere in the pine needles.

"Don't be rude. Introduce yourself to Oscar Weiner."

A thin white scar bisects his left eyebrow. "Take my purse," I tell them. "It's right there in the car. Take all the money."

"Yeah, we'll do that."

"But first I wanna know what's inside those boots," Oscar says. The sour smell is coming from his mouth.

"I don't want any trouble." My voice is controlled. "Take my purse, and we'll forget the whole thing."

"Good-bye?" Oscar reaches down. Scritching severs the darkness—an unmistakable sound. His zipper.

I swing the bag of canisters, connecting with his face. My knee flies up, but the waders restrict my movement. My knee lands against his inner thigh instead, and I swing the bag again. My arm stops midair. I raise my knee again, but it goes nowhere.

"Whoa, whoa!" he says.

I yank my arms. But their grip on my wrists could break bone. My feet paw the ground, the rubber uselessly slipping across the pine needles. Oscar pushes his face into my ear, offering another dose of the putrid aroma.

"That ain't nice," he hisses.

I pull my head back. "Let me go. Please."

"Let you go?"

"I work for the FBI."

Oscar grins. His teeth are gray, the right molar chipped. "Gus, she works for the FBI."

"Never heard that one before."

"I don't want any trouble," I tell them.

"We don't want trouble either." Oscar yanks off the waders. "Now, that's a whole lot better."

I pull back, my spine pressing against the K-Car's door.

"We'll go slow. And if you don't make trouble, we'll let you go."

28

Their Ford Econoline is parked behind the pines. The paint is forest green, with one gray patch above the right wheel. Committing the license plate to memory, I add it to the white scar, the chipped tooth, the name Gus, the possible name Oscar, and the cigarette butts littering the ground. When the van door opens, I see dark brown shag and acoustic foam; I smell rank body odor. Then realize it's mine. The scent of fear, pure fear. My mind fills with prayers so frantic they are wordless.

"Get the tape."

Gus reaches into a plastic tackle box beside the wheel well. Fishing hooks scatter across the top shelf. Below, the gray roll of duct tape. My mind flashes to all the duct-tape cases I've analyzed, and with a wild instinct, I start pulling away from them. Just as suddenly, I stop, pushing back the panic. My only chance to keep my hands free now is to save my fight for later.

Gus rips a swath from the roll.

"Please." The word erupts from my throat. "Please don't do this."

Oscar shakes his head as though disappointed that

he is forced to violate me in ways that will alter my life forever. Gus comes at me with the tape, and I scream, a sound that soars from my spine before Gus slaps the tape across my mouth. My nostrils pull for air, flaring with fear.

"You want me to tape her hands?" he asks Oscar.

"Let's try holding her. It's better like that."

In the next split second, my soul fractures. I stand smelling their odor and at the same time see everything from above. I see my chalk-white face, my frightened eyes darting under the dirty dome light, the desperate breathing that makes the duct tape pooch in and out over my mouth. *Get evidence.* With my fingernails, I scrape the van's barn doors, the slivers of paint slicing into my skin. Gus shoves my arms back, and I rake my fingers against his head, collecting hair. Dead or alive, I will testify.

"Keep her still!" Oscar yells. He throws me on the acoustic foam. I rub my head until it pulls hair out. He climbs on top, and my fingernails rake his skin.

"You wanna be tied up?" Oscar yells. "We can do that."

The doors slam shut. But the dome light stays on. His sweaty face is above me. There is not enough air. Oscar unzips my shorts, and Gus's sweaty fingers tighten around my wrists. Apocine glands. The apocine glands in his hands are depositing evidence on my arms. Thinking about this is better than thinking about Oscar's fingers on my bare stomach. Gus throws his head back, howling. I yank down my arms, rolling left, plunging both hands into the open tackle box. I grab the lures, metal hooks piercing my fingers. I roll back, scratching their faces, aiming for the eyes. My knee connects perfectly this time, and Oscar screams. He falls forward, landing on me, forcing air from my lungs that explodes against the duct tape. My hands swat the air, making the dim light flutter. And then all goes black. My face slams into the wheel well. When I scream, the tape steals the sound.

"I got her, I got her, I got her!" Gus holds my arms again. "Oscar, I got her!"

Oscar is moaning when I hear the gun fire. A cool sensation on my bare stomach tells me I've been shot, and I picture the open wound, bleeding me to death. This is how it ends.

"Get out," the voice growls.

I can't move. Oscar is still on top of me. And Gus holds my arms. I'm hyperventilating but not getting air.

"Get out or I'll blow your heads off."

I recognize the voice. And the man pulling my arms from Gus's limp grasp, shoving Oscar away. I stumble out, yanking off the tape.

DeMott Fielding aims the shotgun into the van. Oscar is curled into a fetal position, moaning. Gus crawls out. Tentatively he watches the barrel following him.

"On the ground," DeMott growls.

Gus hesitates, and DeMott fires. The shot whizzes past Gus's shoulder to the river. After recocking, DeMott shoves Gus down, then pulls Oscar out of the van, throwing him on the ground.

One metal lure is still hooked to my left index finger. I pull it out, tearing the skin, my hands shaking. Grabbing the roll of duct tape, I bind their hands behind their backs. When Oscar's mouth pulls sideways as if

161

he's trying to say something, I roll him over and slap the tape over his mouth.

DeMott's eyes flick from the men to me. "You all right?"

"How did you . . . ?"

"I take back everything I said about that guy Wally. I called your mom's house. He said you came down here. I called your cell phone. You didn't answer."

I nod, then walk to my car, searching the pine needles for my keys. Then I dial 911 and ask for the Charles City County Sheriff. I have to wait for the connection, and I tilt my head back. The night's stars hover close. So close I lift one bloody hand to touch them.

29

I make sure the deputies bag the tackle box, the duct tape, the brown shag, and the acoustic foam, and send it all to the state forensics lab. With sick certainty, I know these things will hold hairs, fibers, and proteins belonging to other women who may or may not still be alive. I tell them to collect soil samples from the tire treads and pop the hubcaps for the older soil inside. It will help pinpoint other locations, if necessary.

My hands have stopped shaking, but the gash in my palm throbs with a hard pulse still full of adrenaline and fight. I give my statement to the Charles City County Sheriff, who gently takes my elbow, leading me to the rescue squad wagon. A young woman cleans the wound with antiseptic solution that stings like a knife. I suck air through my teeth, feeling sudden gratitude that I'm breathing freely again.

When the cruisers pull away, Oscar and Gus are hunched into the backseats. A tow truck follows, pulling the Econoline, and finally the sheriff drives out, lifting his hand to DeMott in that languid wave of country folk. The sheriff will not report DeMott for carrying a firearm, not when the felon's family is the county's largest landholder.

"I'll drive you home," DeMott says.

I shake my head, unable to look at his face. Behind us, mist rises from the riverbank, floating toward the parking lot. I open the K-Car door. On the floorboard, under the driver's seat, is my gun. Snug in its holster.

"At least let me follow you home," he says.

I can't go home. Not like this. I follow DeMott's pickup east on Route 5 until we pull into Weyanoke's drive. In the field a herd of deer stand silhouetted by our headlights before bolting for the woods. And in the mansion's foyer, Mac stands next to her older sister, Jillian. As soon as we come through the door, the women rush forward. DeMott holds up his hand, signaling them to stop. "Everything's fine," he says. "Go back to bed."

But women are equipped with emotional barometers, part of the female spine, and when Mac and Jillian find my eyes, they know. Jillian takes me upstairs to a guest suite where a walnut canopy bed is layered with embroidered silk.

"I've got fresh clothes right here," Jillian says. "And MacKenna's putting on a spread in the sunroom. You'll have to forgive her, Raleigh. It'll probably look like she's throwing a party. My sister responds to every crisis by cooking food." She holds up linen trousers and a blouse green as weathered copper. "I also have pajamas. In case you just want to sleep."

Most people would say Jillian is not as pretty as Mac. Where Mac's eyes are luminous as tiger's-eye, Jillian's brown eyes are peaty like her father's. Her hair doesn't

164

have that high black shine either. But there is no denying which sister is the true beauty. I watch as Jillian folds and unfolds the clothing, laying white socks on the pink silk bed. "Clean socks always make me feel better, isn't that weird?" She pauses. "I'm sorry this happened, Raleigh. But I'm glad DeMott was there. He's a good guy."

"I can't argue with you. He saved my life tonight."

"We come across as arrogant. The Fieldings aren't exactly shy and retiring. But with all my heart I mean this: we're here when you need us. And if you never want to mention this again, there will be enough food downstairs to feed an army." She smiles in a bittersweet way. "Mac will be a wonderful wife. Her greatest strength is glossing over tragedy."

"I just wanted to get cleaned up before going home," I tell her, then ask about her parents, whether they'll be downstairs too. I'm not ready to see Harrison Fielding.

"They're both gone," she says. "Mother's at Kingsmill, that spa in Williamsburg? She hasn't reconciled herself to sixty. And Daddy's attending some conference in Philadelphia about garbage."

"Garbage?"

She smiles. "Don't you dare say 'garbage' around him, but Daddy's convinced the Fielding future is landfills. He's turning his real estate into landfills. He opened one in Richmond last year. You should have heard the arguments! Mother said, 'First, we aid and abet Yankees, and now we're literal trash.'"

For a short moment, I laugh, and it feels like I'm dreaming. When Jillian leaves, I start the shower and then stare at myself in the gilded mirror. My chestnut hair teased into weird nests and red blotches disfigure my face. A purple bruise spreads over my left temple, where the scratches from the brick building look renewed, crimson once again. But the worst is my eyes. They are too round, startled. And I've seen my eyes like this once before, after my father died. This is the face of someone who suddenly realizes some crucial fence, some barrier holding back the dark edges of life, is gone.

In the shower I have to remind myself that the evidence is already collected, that it's okay to wash my hair three times, and scrub my skin raw. On the upholstered bench beside the vanity, Jillian's laid a thick white robe. I dress in the linen pants, the blouse, and stare at myself in the mirror again. My image keeps shifting. I see the duct tape, their dirty fingernails, his hands on my bare stomach, and suddenly I'm staring at the countertop, thinking, *That's not granite, it's magmatite. Partially melted rock.* I run my hand over the cool stone, seeing slivers of mica glint in the overhead light. *Mica . . . Micah.* My father's soothing baritone reciting the crucial words. *What does the Lord require of you? To act justly, to love mercy, to walk humbly with your God.*

When I cover my face, the salt tears sting my hands.

Jillian and Mac clear out plates from the sunroom, offer hugs, wish me good night. DeMott remains in the sunroom, where the buttery lamplight falls across the black windows that face the river. "Let's get some air," he says.

The night is soft, warm as God's breath. But I shiver. High clouds blow across the black sky, moving like moon-lit scarves. DeMott's walking stick thump-thumps the ground every other step. I want to turn, run for the house, when his callused hand takes mine—he takes the good hand.

"Thank you," I tell him again.

"Thank Wally," he says. "By the way, did you read my note yet?"

When I don't say anything, he says, "That's okay."

The grass, pearly with dew, tickles my ankles.

"Raleigh, I want to tell you something."

"DeMott—"

"You tend to get stuck in the past."

"Pardon?"

"Well, you do."

I let go of his hand. "Do you see where you live?"

"We'll talk about me another time. Right now I see that brave face of yours, and I know what you'll do after tonight. You'll muscle your way through this . . . this . . . *thing* that almost happened all the while deep down, it will disturb you. You'll keep pushing your feelings away. That's how you get stuck in the past."

I turn and walk back toward the mansion.

He runs after me. "I'm sorry about tonight. I'm sorry about that bad date in high school. I should have said that before now."

"That night never happened."

"You see?" he exclaims. "You didn't even do anything wrong. You had too much to drink and passed out."

"And woke up next to you with my clothes off."

"Nothing happened."

So he says. It was a bad idea to come here. I should have gone home, hid from Nadine, sent a thank-you note to DeMott addressed to this strange historic preserve of Fieldings. Behind me, DeMott runs to catch up.

"Raleigh, you need to forget the past."

"Is that so?" I stop, turning to him. "That's helpful, coming from someone who lives in a Civil War museum."

He drops his head. Behind us, pre-dawn light is already bright as fire opals burning against the ashy morning. The white T-shaped grapevines stutter down to the river like crosses.

Inside the house, I collect my clothing and leave a note for the girls. DeMott waits in the foyer, then walks me to the K-Car. "You do what you have to do," he says.

I toss my dirty clothes in the backseat. "I appreciate your help tonight. I don't know what—"

He lifts his hand again. "Don't say anything. Ever."

As dawn breaks I drive away, listening to the fine gravel strike the undercarriage. DeMott appears in my rearview mirror. Standing on Weyanoke's manicured front lawn, he raises one hand, holding it there until my car is out of sight.

30

Later that morning, the gilded dome of the U.S. Capitol blazes like a flame against Washington's heavy gray haze. I park under Bureau headquarters and take the elevator to the third floor.

It was 5:00 a.m. when I left Weyanoke, nearly 6:00 when I reached the Richmond office. Except for some security staff and four grouchy agents who pulled night surveillance, the office was empty. I typed out the necessary forms, made copies for Allene, asking her to send the 1B numbers and barcodes to my email, then climbed back in the K-Car with a cup of coffee and drove north, hitting commuter traffic at its usual slow crawl.

At some point, I will have to sleep. My eyes sting, my skin itches. And as I walk down the hall to mineralogy, the fluorescent lighting makes my vision vibrate. Eric looks up from his desk. "Raleigh, what are you doing here?"

I slide the custody forms and evidence toward him, and he reads—what needs to be tested in this soil, the paper trash, the comparison samples. "I need another set of Ks," I tell him, my voice hoarse with insomnia.

"Compare this soil to what I collected from the roof. Then compare it with the shoes."

He turns toward me, slowly, a man expecting to be startled by what he will see. "Raleigh," he says carefully, "what happened to you?"

"Nothing."

"I could deal with some scratches on your face, but this—"

"The case is an expedite, Eric."

He nods, making an agreement with somebody out of their mind, beyond reason. "I've got a huge lineup in front of this," he says.

"Okay, I'll start the wash." The room spins like a top, but I manage to sign the evidence control and chain of command sheets, notifying whoever checks later that I performed preliminary lab tests, because I still hold some rights to the lab and Eric is watching my every move. Let the defense attorneys try; I'm clear as crystal. I deposit the soil samples from each canister into separate glass cylinders, then lower them into an ultrasonic bath with a low-sudsing detergent. For several seconds, my mind struggles for the soap's name. Calgon. That's it. We used to laugh in here and say, "Calgon, take me away." I hit the switch, sending ultrasonic waves pulsing through the water, humming like a washing machine. In a more simplified way, my mother's jewelry cleaner works on the same principle of ultrasonic energy knocking debris from solid mineral. Since the wash takes thirty minutes, I lay my head on the empty desk and decide to close my eyes.

"Raleigh, it's dry."

For one split second, I feel that blissful sensation, rising from well-deserved sleep. But just as suddenly, the good feeling vanishes, replaced by panic. "How long was I out?"

"Two hours," Eric says. "The samples are dry."

Under the heat lamp, the soil samples are separated and marked. Eric's brought in the dried roof soil too, setting it near the others for comparison. "The colors are all close."

It sounds too elementary to be scientific, but color identification is one of the most crucial aspects of forensic mineralogy. Cleaned of debris, a mineral's true color becomes evident—yellow, red, green, blue, purple—all standardized on the Munsell Color Chart. Carrying the samples to the north window for the truest natural light, I see both river soils match the roof sample soil. Taupe green with gray undertones.

"Try the scope," Eric says.

Under the stereoscope, I set magnification on 10X and peer through the lens at the three-dimensional highlights, seeing the differences in micron sizes. Some of the South Anna soil grains are too large to match the roof soil. But the James River sample is a dead ringer on size. At ten times magnification, pyrite's perpendicular crystal structure looks like tumbling sugar cubes. Eric has already opened the mineralogy manual to pyrite's description.

"In the James River sample," he says, "you get a match to the roof soil in color, texture, and size. But the question is, is it the same pyrite? Plain ferrous sulfide, or FeS_2, or even some other ferrous sulfide?"

"Pyrite in the roof soil, pyrite in the James River soil. Same size grains. They're a match."

"You're forgetting how deceitful ferrous sulfide can be, Raleigh. So let me remind you, before some defense attorney hires an independent geologist and pays him huge sums of money so he can tell the jury, 'Ladies and gentlemen, the common name for pyrite is fool's gold, and that's exactly what the FBI has here, fool's gold.'" He closes the manual. "You want results, Raleigh, but you haven't nailed this K. You'll need X-ray diffractions."

X-ray diffraction means we shoot radiation through the mineral, producing an angle of diffracted light. Every crystal structure produces a distinct X-ray pattern, measured and quantified, but the test requires time and skill, and I'm in no shape to run it this morning. And I'm on thin ice if I do, from a legal standpoint, because it's not some preliminary test. And Eric has no time.

He points to the heat lamp. "Now, for the acrylamide." He rolls his chair to the samples. "The acrylamide had polymers pressed flat."

"Foot pressure?" I ask.

"Doubtful. The mineral sheets were created in the manufacturing process, flat before they got in the shoe treads. But when I added water, the roof sample just exploded. Watch this."

His hands palsy, dropping the distilled water into the petri dishes, creating dark puddles. The detective's shoe sample expands so fast it looks shot with steroids. Meanwhile, the sample from Holmes's shoes expands, but only slightly. And nothing happens to the James River sample: an inert puddle.

172

My head is foggy, but I sense the gentle letdown. If I was asleep that long, Eric had time to run every one of these tests. He already knows the answer. This demonstration is for my benefit. "How much acrylamide are we talking about?" I ask.

"The soil from the South Anna River, near the paper plant, had enough acrylamide to launch an environmentalist hissy fit," he says. "Maybe one-millionth of 1 percent. But the roof sample? There's enough acrylamide to cause permanent damage to the human nervous system."

I let it sink in. "No acrylamide in the James River sample?"

He sets the petri dish on the counter.

"Be straight with me," I tell him.

"None. The river sample doesn't match the roof soil, Raleigh. But the good news is the shoes match each other. Just one pair has more acrylamide than the other."

I take a deep breath, sinking back in the chair.

"The real key here," Eric says, "is that the acrylamide was pressed flat for manufacturing. It's thin, but absorbs a massive amount of water. If you can figure out where that comes from, you've got your location."

I could do that, if I had time.

———

As I'm walking out of FBI headquarters, my cell phone rings. It's Phaup. I let the phone take the message and cross E Street to Starbucks. I need more coffee. Then I keep walking. Down near the corner, Lady Jay Wigs is still here, sandwiched between the ninety-nine-cent dry cleaner and the Korean bakery. Today Lady Jay herself is in the shop, adjusting a red pillbox hat with grosgrain ribbon.

"You probably don't remember me," I begin.

"Sure do." She points across the street to the Bureau. "You're the science girl. Where you been?"

I explain my move to Richmond, that I live with my mother now. "She still wearing my hats?" Lady Jay asks.

When I worked in the lab, I used to bring home hats for Nadine, as much as to see my father's face light up when she tried them on. "She wears them to church," I tell her.

"Best place for them." She points to my cheekbone. "Man do that to you?" Lady Jay always did do more than sell hats. In constant "ministry" to every woman who walks through the door, she goes straight to the most personal questions.

I reach up, touching the bruise, the skin hot and tender. Lady Jay offers me a green felt hat with a thick black veil. Not my style. Not Nadine's, either. But I find a pale straw number, blue blossoms decorating the brim. When I dip my head, the hat undulates like a stingray. Lady Jay tilts it, just so, concealing the bruise, then rings up the purchase.

I drive south toward Richmond, the day so humid that every bit of blue is leached from the sky. South of Fredericksburg, I pick up Route 1 and follow the asphalt ribbon through the verdant farms. My radio picks up a country-western station that comes in and out while I tell myself that yesterday was just another day. No need to think about it anymore. Let it go. Move on.

But the country song tells me the truth: my mind's got a mind of its own.

174

31

When I look through the kitchen window, I see my mother sitting at the pine table, her odd acrostics lining white paper. Dozens of words race down the page in a torrent of non sequiturs. I watch her work the letters, standing so still Madame continues to slumber under the table. I want to fall into my mother's arms, tearfully tell her what happened last night. I want to hear her lilting voice say everything is all right now, the bad men are gone, gone, gone away and will never return.

I open the door. Madame gives a short bark.

"Raleigh Ann!" my mother exclaims, turning over the tablet. She pulls off her reading glasses. "Wally said you were out of town."

Madame's tail thumps against my leg. "I was. I brought you a souvenir."

"Oh, isn't it lovely!" The hat's wide brim falls over her black curls, flopping on her shoulders with languid ease. She tilts her head this way and that, catching her reflection in the glass door. "It's simply perfect," she declares. "Thank you."

Great scientists have boiled the universe down to

atomic structure. And sometimes I can almost see how God might use atoms to build this grand design, sort of like divine building blocks. People, plants, animals, and rocks—we're built through the power of atoms. But it isn't the whole story. Environment exerts its influences, even altering appearances in such a way it's difficult to remember those basic atomic structures. If given room to grow, for instance, quartz will form perfect hexagonal crystals. But trapped inside a metamorphic vein, compressed by heat and pressure while still fluid, quartz turns into an indistinct white mass, mimicking whatever shape surrounds it.

My family gave me plenty of room to grow. But it did not allow me to break one distinct boundary. Much as I felt the desire, I could not ask so much of someone with so many needs. Comfort was never my mother's role; comfort was my father's role. And now, though he's passed on, the basic family structure remains. I can't ask her.

"The hat looks great on you," I say.

"I'll wear it to the camp." The floppy brim makes her appear lighthearted. But her eyes betray another mood. "Raleigh, you don't look quite right."

"I'm tired. That's all."

"Is that—do I?—oh, my lands! That's a *bruise* on your face, Raleigh Ann!"

I reach up, trying to cover it with my hand. "I walked into a door."

"A door?"

"Yes. I was . . . I was rushing around the office, and I turned the wrong way. Right into the door."

"Well, bless your heart, that looks just awful." Barefoot, she pads over to the refrigerator for her box of medicinals. "We'll put some arnica on that right away."

Welcome to Nadine's herbal pharmacy.

"Hold still," she tells me. "It's cold, but that keeps the swelling down too."

The kitchen chair's frayed fibers poke into the back of my legs. "What does this stuff do?"

"It gets rid of bruises, silly. Why else would I be putting it on your bruise?" Her fingertips tap my tender skin, sending lightning bolts of pain through my head. But I hold still. I hold back. And Nadine hums softly. It's a hymn I can't place. No, she should not hear my troubles. She cannot. But she can administer salves. And serve tempeh bacon and inform me that my circadian rhythms are off. And if these were her only forms of comfort, I accepted them.

"'There Is a Balm in Gilead'?"

"Yes." She straightens, smiling tenderly. "Do you remember the words?"

"Probably not."

She starts tapping my temple, this time on the beat. "Sometimes I feel discourrrrraged, and think my worrrk's in vain, but then the Holy Spirrrrrrrit, revives my soul again . . ."

Madame howls—my mother sings off-key—but when the dog barks again, jumping at the door, I turn and see DeMott Fielding on the patio. Nadine squeals, clattering over, opening the door with both palms like somebody who just got a manicure.

"DeMott Fielding!" she exclaims. "I am so glad to see

you. I need a witness." She points at me. "Look at my daughter. Look at her! Do you see that mark on her eye?" She shakes her head, and the hat does all sorts of gymnastics. "She walked into a door!"

"It looks pretty bad, Mrs. Harmon."

"You know what she needs?" She looks up from under the brim.

"That hat?"

"Oh, you." She swats his arm. "She needs a date. Raleigh Ann needs to get out, live a little. All she does is work. What kind of life is that?"

"Mom—"

"She's young, she's beautiful!"

"I agree with you," DeMott says.

"You hear, Raleigh? He agrees with me."

"What a surprise."

She turns back to him. "Here I was so worried about Raleigh, and all the while the good Lord was sending you over to cheer us up." She puts the tube of cold goo back in her box, wiping her hands on a towel. "DeMott, please tell your family hello. If you'll excuse me, I have to go put my hat in water." She trills her ringed fingers. Madame follows her out of the room.

DeMott watches her go. "You could not be more different," he finally says.

"That's occurred to me."

He holds up the paper bag. "Fresh scones from Mac. She's still worried about you."

We drink iced tea that looks suspiciously pale, perhaps laced with some herbal remedy that I warn DeMott about. We eat in silence. My last meal was twelve hours

178

ago, also prepared by Mac. After two scones, I feel strong enough to tell him, "I read your note."

"Forget it," he says.

"You said it was urgent."

"It seemed urgent at the time. I probably just wanted a reason to talk to you." He picks up our plates and carries them to the sideboard. When he comes back to the table, he gently brushes the hair from my forehead. Suddenly, he pulls his hand away, looking horrified. "What is that?"

I hand him a napkin. "It's my mother's way of saying she's sorry I got hurt."

"It feels like . . . snot."

"I understand. Now, what's the urgent news?"

"Maybe nothing. I just wanted to tell you I knew that guy, Detective Falcon, who fell off the roof. He was tough."

"This was for methamphetamine?"

He nods. "Mac and Jillian kept telling me I was an addict. But what did they know, the little princesses. I stopped speaking to them, I stopped speaking to everybody. And one night I'm driving through Jackson Ward for a score, and this cute girl comes up to my car. She's going to help me, right? Next thing I know, Falcon's grilling me down at the station until my father got his lawyer in there."

My mother sent all the newspaper stories to Mt. Holyoke so I could read about DeMott Fielding's fall from grace. The stories always reminded readers how he belonged to those illegitimate Southerners. And in the margins, my mother jotted Bible verses and always, always, the same three words: "Pray for him."

179

"I went into treatment after that," he says. "And I helped the police bust some labs around Richmond. Falcon's testimony at my sentencing really cut my time."

In a city where entire neighborhoods refuse to speak to the police, cooperation is a powerful bargaining chip. Cooperation is why Milky Lewis sculpts giraffes at VCU while his former cohorts mop urine off the floors at Lorton Prison. "Did you ever talk to Falcon again?"

He wrote Falcon a thank-you letter, but the detective never contacted him. Falcon did, however, call Harrison Fielding, he says. "He wanted to start a chain of security firms. Franchises, all run by retired inner-city cops. Dad liked the idea, especially since our buildings get vandalized all the time."

I pause, the dots suddenly connecting. "Just how much did your father like this idea?"

"He gave him two hundred thousand dollars."

When my mouth drops open, DeMott says, "Hey, that's nothing. He already pays that, for insurance and upkeep on those empty Southside buildings. Falcon even offered to manage Dad's properties for free, until he could pay back the money."

I remember the building, that second day after the men died. No windows were broken. The double-door entrance intact, the glass grated with steel wire. Locks unbroken. "Nobody broke into that factory."

"What?"

Nobody broke into that factory. Because Falcon had the keys. I stare at DeMott. "Somehow, your father failed to mention he knew the detective."

"That's why I wrote you the note, Raleigh. When you left

180

Weyanoke that day, I asked him if he told you about the security arrangements. He said the newspaper claimed the detective was on street patrol. Dad worried that if he brought up the moonlighting job, it would mess up death benefits for the family."

"Lying to an FBI agent is a federal crime." I get up, start washing the dishes, the hot water seeping into the cuts on my fingers. The wounds scream.

DeMott stands next to me. "Listen, Harrison Fielding is all about self-preservation. But he really did worry about the widow."

I turn off the water, taking a deep breath. "Anything else your father 'forgot' to tell me?"

"Probably," he says.

32

Thursday morning I turn into the James River correctional facility, where the Blue Ridge foothills form an indigo spine across Goochland County. I pass the warden's plantation house and park outside the concrete block buildings out back among an assortment of vehicles, including a green school bus belonging to the police academy.

Inside, twelve FBI agents fill pistol magazines with Winchester ammo, wearing ear protection and safety glasses. Since my wraparound sunglasses have safety lenses, I won't have to explain the bruise right now.

Every three months FBI agents take mandatory firearms training because the Bureau wants to make sure we can still handle our weapons—the weapons we're not supposed to leave in our cars. I pack the Glock's magazine with cartridges as firearms instructor DuWayne Smith explains today's drills. Then I take my position on the twenty-five-yard mark. Our paper targets shaped like heads and torsos hang at the other end of the gallery. When DuWayne gives the signal, we fire. I squint my left eye, and the bruise throbs. Pain throws my first score, which wouldn't even qualify for agent training. We fire three more rounds in various positions—standing, kneeling, lying on our stomachs—and the air fills with gunpowder. The shell casings ping the concrete in a tender counterpoint to pistol blast. Finally I'm shooting well, not one bullet straying from the kill zone. I know why.

DuWayne sends us outside for the last drill. Every four minutes, another agent bolts for the door. In the hot sun outside, we listen to the gunfire in the building. When my turn comes, I sprint for the door, pulling my weapon. My target moves across the gallery like a paper ghost. I aim for his head. Nail it. I run to the wooden barrier, taking my position, but the target turns sideways, signaling me to hold fire, adversary is not an immediate threat. My index finger rests lightly on the trigger. When the target flips, I fire twice, then sprint diagonally to the fifteen-yard line, changing magazines on the way. I nail the next four marks and repeat on the seven-yard and three-yard targets.

The kill zone is shredded.

DuWayne's firearms assistant Leatty whistles. "Not bad." Leatty's the same age as John Breit, only this guy isn't burned out. "You're almost hitting one hundred, Raleigh. In two minutes, forty-four seconds. I wish every agent shot like this."

I carry my destroyed target outside, ready to gloat, ready for redemption, for something that will heal the howling lament within my heart. So what if I left my gun in the car—look at this! But my eyes start to burn, and the air fills with an odd chemical odor. By then, it's too late. My throat is in flames.

John Breit is yelling. "How many times do we have to tell you? Don't use the Mace when we're out here!"

I can't see John, because I can't open my eyes. This has happened before—too often—when the police academy instructors liberally apply Mace to the trainees to demonstrate the effects firsthand. Floating on the summer air in noxious clouds, the chemical strikes everyone within a wide radius.

"You idiot!" John yells. "Now we're blind!"

I blink, trying to find John. The police trainees are standing behind him, moaning as they try to wash the poison from their eyes under the building's spigot. But water won't help. I know, I've tried. My colleagues have taken cover behind the green school bus, blocking the killing breeze. They curse the cops. And I stand in the bright sun, holding my ace target. I let the tears roll.

33

Back in the carriage house, I crank up the air conditioner, take a long cool shower, rinsing my still-burning eyes, and evaluate my face in the mirror above the pedestal sink. The bruise is purple.

In the cedar closet, I find my grandmother's makeup box. Selma Harmon only wore Charles of the Ritz face powder. As I dab the soft talc on my bruise, her scent rises, warm as vanilla, soft as rain. But the powder has so much pink the bruise looks worse after camouflage. When my cell phone rings, I walk into the living room and check the caller ID. It's not Phaup, so I pick up.

Mike Rodriguez says, "The hair follicle doesn't match either of the deceased, and none of their clothing matches what you brought in on the First Aid tape."

I try to clear my mind as he explains that the red fibers on the building aren't from Holmes's shoes. The blue threads are rip-stop nylon. "Like a windbreaker, and neither of these guys was wearing a windbreaker."

"Mike, I collected that hair and those fibers right off the brick. It's got to match these guys."

"That's why I examine evidence," he says. "It is what it is. Good luck, Raleigh."

———

For some miraculous reason, my car radio picks up an actual station on the way to the office. Hank Williams feels lonesome, and the DJ claims it's ninety-two degrees, if you don't add the humidity. I rehearse my speech for Phaup, but when I get to her office, her door is closed. She's busy with another agent. Maybe I should believe in luck.

I start to head back to my desk. Phaup's secretary takes off her dictation headset. "She'll be done in one minute," Claudia says.

"Okay, I'll come back."

"No, really. One minute," she explains. "Her upper limit is twenty-three minutes. This meeting is going on twenty-two. If you leave, it will take you four minutes to get upstairs, but you won't reach your desk for another seven because you haven't been in the office. You'll stop and talk, then you'll spend another five minutes getting back down here because she's been calling you and wants to see you immediately. Save me from having to call you again, because"—Claudia pauses, turning toward Phaup's office—"here she is."

The agent steps out, cradling a brown accordion file under one arm. His name is Hugh Blundell. Former CPA, he works White Collar. "All yours." Hugh winks.

Claudia puts the headset back on, dropping her voice. "Get it over with."

———

186

Like any good investigator, I'm always surreptitiously glancing around Phaup's office for clues. But there are none. No family portraits, no pictures of pets. No memorable vacation photos. Just one small Navajo rug between her desk and the club chairs. Phaup's last position, in Albuquerque.

"I've been trying to reach you." She points to the chair.

"Yes, ma'am."

"I realize agents screen calls. And if you're busy at the very moment I'm calling, fine. But two days is too long out of touch."

"Yes, ma'am."

"That won't happen again. Now, give me an update on the 44."

I tell her both men carried a distinct soil in their shoes, meaning they were in an identical location before colliding on the roof. Also, my suspicion is that Hamal Holmes was linked to a cold case the detective was working. Moreover, the detective had keys to the building. I'm about to explain Rodriguez's report on the hairs and fibers when she interrupts me.

"I got a call this morning."

I brace myself. More *People* magazine inquiries.

"The Charles City Sheriff was asking how we want to prosecute those guys who attacked you."

I open my mouth.

She says, "If we assert they attacked you because you're an FBI agent, it's a federal crime. Any suggestions, Agent Harmon?"

My voice croaks. "I was taking soil samples."

187

"What in the . . . that's how you plan to resolve this case?"

I explain again, that we're talking a specific location for both men previous to the roof. So specific it's a fingerprint.

She walks around her desk, pulling at her skirt. "I'm suspending you for two weeks."

I didn't hear that. "What?"

"You're suspended for leaving your weapon in the car."

"How—" I stop.

"You got lucky. It doesn't always turn out that way. Let me tell you a story." She describes two agents on stakeout, sitting in the car for hours until their backsides are aching and stomachs are growling. But there's an Indian restaurant down the block, and they've been smelling curry all night. One agent runs in to get some takeout. "But as the agent's paying, a man walks into the restaurant with a gun," she says calmly. "He tells everyone to hit the floor and proceeds to empty the cash register. The proprietor fights back. The perp shoots him dead." She pauses. "This is a sad story. But the real question is: why didn't the agent neutralize the situation?"

"Because the agent didn't have a gun."

"Yes, the agent left the weapon in the car."

I nod. "It won't happen again."

"No, it won't. You will never forget that weapon again. The suspension is effective today."

"Today?"

"I'm giving the case to John Breit."

John, who will close immediately.

"You failed to take proper precautions, Raleigh. You forgot your gun and you didn't take backup. I'm writing a letter of censure for your personnel file."

I wait for the nightmare to end. But the monster won't go away. It only grows bigger.

"What were you really doing out there?" she asks.

"I told you, taking soil samples." I explain: I didn't ask for backup because she wanted the case resolved quickly and I couldn't wait for somebody else's schedule to clear. "There was plenty of light when I started."

"But some rednecks decided you were an easy mark. Guess what? You were." She crosses her arms. "Tell me the requirement for firearms."

I recite it like a schoolgirl. "Armed on duty, in the office, or while conducting FBI business."

"What part of that don't you understand?"

"I understand it all. Ma'am."

"I'm recommending OPR look into this."

She can't be serious. OPR, the Office of Professional Responsibility. No matter what their final verdict is, their investigation means a permanent black mark on my record, affecting the rest of my career with the Bureau.

"It won't happen again," I repeat. "Suspension, letter of censure, that's plenty."

"What if the sheriff had called to inform me your body was in the morgue?" she says. "Lock up your firearm. Take your vehicle home but don't drive it after that. You will report back here in fifteen days. In the meantime, OPR will be in touch."

When I stand, my head spins. The walk across her office takes ten years. But it's time enough to figure out some things, and when I turn around, she's back at her desk, lost in her mass of papers.

"You were that agent," I say. "The one in the restaurant."

She doesn't even bother looking up. "And I never forgot my gun again."

34

I park the K-Car several blocks off Monument Avenue and walk the alley to the carriage house's back entrance. My answering machine offers two messages: Wally, asking about my schedule for the weekend (boy, did I have a surprise for him), and DeMott, wondering about that date my mother proposed.

There's a distant rumble in the sky, charcoal clouds looming. But I've got that jangly heartbeat in a bad way. Quickly I change my clothes, sneaking back down the alley. I jog the Boulevard, past the Daughters of the Confederacy headquarters where all the iron cannons still point north. Two miles later on Libbie Avenue, I run a loop around my high school alma mater, St. Catherine's School. A place where failure was not an option. And now failure has come.

When lightning finally cracks, I cut down Somerset, ducking into the West End neighborhood. I find the lowest, widest oak, pressing my back against its trunk. The sky opens. Lightning tears rain's vessel, and water pounds the street, pummeling the leaves, drowning the gardens. The sound is like a stadium filled with applause.

I watch drivers pull over to the roadside, hazard lights blinking, their wipers uselessly whipping across the windshield. For one long extended moment, Richmond stops dead in its tracks. Rain beats the city into submission.

And then, just as suddenly as it came, the storm fades. The rain stops. Thunder leaves. Cars pull back onto the road, sloshing puddles already draining into the grates. Birds chirp.

I start my run toward home, the sky blue and black with spent clouds. The darkness tricks streetlights into turning on too soon. As I run down Grove Avenue, the lights flash against the puddles, turning water white. After such a hard rain, the air smells like clover and the city feels freshly baptized, its sins forgiven though never forgotten.

When I pass the Daughters of the Confederacy headquarters, I slow to a walk, staring at the cannons. Richmond was defeated, but it remained bowed. A defiant city, begrudging, acknowledging its troubled past but refusing to make a wasteland of a bygone era. Cruelty and affliction do not deny grace and gentility, or the hope of salvation. Down Monument Avenue, I see General Lee and Traveller, glistening with water.

For better or worse, this city is part of me. I can no more turn my back on Richmond than the Daughters could reverse those cannons. Despite its troubles, its wounds that stretch back centuries, Richmond is my home. It is my family. My heart. And asking me to neglect it is like asking the General to ride into eternity facing North.

It won't happen. It can't happen.

35

The next morning, I cross the courtyard and find Wally at the kitchen table, reading the gossip column.

"Where's Nadine?" I ask.

"Building an ark."

"Seriously."

He drops the paper. "Seriously? She got up in the middle of the night and made some weirdo herbal tea that stunk up the place. Smell gave me nightmares. I came downstairs, thinking I was dying. She just smiled and told me to go back to bed, sweet dreams. I got up an hour ago. She was sound asleep in her room, Madame with her, and I chose to greet the day despite feeling the way tofu looks."

I pour a cup of coffee. The only bread in the house is something called Spelt. Worse than the name, the bag insists there is no flour in this bread. I drop two stiff slices into the toaster and explain to Wally that I've been suspended for two weeks. And I don't want Nadine to know.

I hear the newspaper rustle. The toaster pops.

"This because of what happened at the river?" he asks.

The bread has the hearty appearance of meatless meatloaf, which my mother has served. "It's disciplinary action. I made a mistake, a serious mistake. Now I have to deal with the consequences."

"What a load," he says. "You should fight it."

"Don't worry," I tell him. It's already been decided.

———

In the cold case file loaned to me by Detective Greene, I find several small photographs of a girl named Cecille Saunders. Documents note Cecille Saunders's career in prostitution, beginning at age fifteen. Child Protective Services notes Cecille's father is "Not Known" and a younger sister lives at home. The mother works sporadically for the Southside post office. Cecille was also picked up for possession of crack. Not long after, the medical examiner's report completes the documentary: Cecille Saunders, age sixteen, shot in the back of the head execution style in Chimbarazo Park by a .38.

I drive the Benz to Southside, to the Jefferson Davis Apartments. Steam rises from the black roof as the morning sun evaporates last night's heavy rain. Next to the building, four children play on a swing set, the metal legs bucking out of the mud with their trajectories.

Apartment 109A shares an alcove with another apartment, 109B, which has an eviction notice from the sheriff's office nailed to the frame. I knock twice on 109A. Then harder, lifting my fist to knock a third time when a woman answers. Tall and skinny, she wears an enormous T-shirt advertising Adidas tennis shoes. Orange hair haloes her narrow face. I introduce myself as Raleigh Harmon, but I don't add "FBI." The woman seems very tired, possibly high. Judging by the aroma wafting from her apartment, my guess is she's high.

"I don't know where those people went," she tells me. "I got enough trouble of my own to worry about my neighbors."

It takes me a moment to understand what she's referring to. "Ma'am, I'm not here about the eviction. I'm here about your daughter."

"Ain't seen her neither. She flew off somewheres last week, maybe even the week before. Left me with her kids."

These are powerful drugs. "Your daughter Cecille ran away last week?"

She scowls. "I'm talkin' about Cherry."

"Cherry . . ."

"Cherainc?" she says peevishly. "My daughter Cheraine? Who else would I be talking about?"

Oh, right. The younger sister, mentioned in the file. "Your daughter is Cheraine."

"Not no more she's not. That girl done took off for the last time. I'm supposed to keep her kids, while she has herself a good time? Uh-uh. Who does she think I am, Mary Poppins?" She narrows the eyes. "But you asked about Ceelie."

Maybe she's not high. "Yes, ma'am, I'm looking into the circumstances surrounding her death."

She stares at me levelly. "You know something, tell me. My heart done broke over that girl."

195

I show her Detective Falcon's police photo, and she smiles as if surprised by a good memory. "Detective Mike. But he dead now. And Hamal," she says slowly. "I don't know how Cherry's gonna take that news."

"Your daughter knew Mr. Holmes?"

She tosses her head toward the playground. "Them's his kids."

I turn. The children twist the swing chains, releasing themselves into vertigo helixes. Not two miles from here, in the house on Castlewood Street, the widow has more children. When I ask their ages, she scratches her head. Her fingernails sparkle with pink polish.

"Hamal Jr. is nine. He came along the year after Ceelie died. And know who buried my girl decent? Hamal. That's right. He paid for her coffin." The tears appear suddenly, slipping down her ashen cheeks.

"Mr. Holmes knew Cecille too?"

"No, he just wanted to help. That boy always took care of people. That's how come everybody's so upset, especially with him dying like that."

"Do you believe the detective threw him?"

She shakes her head. "But it don't matter what I believe. Truth's got its own way of going."

I ask more about the funeral arrangements Holmes paid for, and she steps into the apartment, returning with a paper fan consisting of rounded cardstock glued to a tongue depressor. The twenty-third Psalm is written on one side, the other advertises Hope Eternal Funeral Home. When I thank Mrs. Saunders for her time, she nods vaguely, waving the fan through the humid air, blowing back the wet streams that carve her cheeks.

The red awning at the Hope Eternal Funeral Home is frayed and dripping with remnants of last night's rain. Black iron bars cover the windows, and though the name implies infinite optimism, the atmosphere inside feels like every other funeral home—weirdly maudlin and spooky.

I knock on an office door, and when no one answers, lift the door latch and step onto an ocean of lapis-colored carpeting. A short thin man appears holding a cigarette.

"I was looking for the funeral director," I tell him.

"Douglass Canes." He moves the cigarette to his left hand and shoots out the right palm. I introduce myself by name, explaining that law enforcement agencies are looking into the circumstances surrounding several recent deaths.

His brown eyes widen. "I haven't broken any laws."

"Yes, sir, I'm sure that's true." This place is so quiet every word sounds louder than it should. "Harnal Holmes died two weeks ago."

"Yes, the family was heartbroken about the closed casket, but by the time we received the body from the medical examiner, there wasn't much we could do."

I've read the coroner's report. It described "insipient brain contusions" erupting across the men's faces, and "contrecoup contusions," meaning the brain ricocheted forward and swelled their features to gross proportions. "Some years ago, Mr. Holmes paid for a funeral, for a girl named Cecille Saunders."

"Oh, I wouldn't be at liberty to discuss that." He looks around for an ashtray, then taps the ash into his left palm.

"Mr. Canes, I'm sure your reputation for guarding information is excellent. But Mr. Holmes is dead."

"My obligations go beyond this life. My services are *eternal*."

And search warrants are public, I explain. Public record means the newspaper can report the information, letting people know his funeral home is being investigated. Or, he and I can keep the secret.

This time, when Douglass Canes smiles, his narrow mouth is laced with resentment. In a low purr, he says, "Well, if you really believe I can help."

36

The gym's tall windows welcome the hot sun. It shines
on the boys jumping rope, swaddled in heavy clothing.
Nylon ropes nick the linoleum with a steady rhythm,
like metronomes set for a death march.

But subtropical heat does not bother Ray Frey. His
dingy sweats are bone-dry. "You're back." He grunts.
"Now what?"

I ask whether he knew Hamal Holmes paid for funerals of strangers.

"I told you about Coretta Scott King," he says. "Hamal
was a great kid, smart, but there were so many screws
loose you could hear them rattle."

I explain further. After my visit to the funeral home,
I cross-checked the names with Detective Greene at the
Richmond P.D. The names all belong to cold cases. Every
single one. Elvin Johnson, a drug dealer beaten to death
in Jackson Ward. Quaniece Blue, an AIDS-infected prostitute whose body was found decomposing in a dumpster
off East Broad Street. And Tiny Walters, a pedophile who
walked away from prosecution on a technicality—Tiny
was later found mutilated on a Southside playground.

There were more, many more, each life as riddled with evil as the next, and each death as bone-silent as dark family secrets. These were the ice-cold cases nobody would talk about.

But Hamal Holmes paid for every funeral. Most of the time, the mortician kept the secret.

"I have a hunch the detective wanted to talk to Holmes that day," I tell Ray Frey.

He turns back to the boys. They jump with closed eyes, the sweat dripping from lean dark faces that are lifted like penitents in painful prayer.

"I don't know nothing," he says.

"Did you know about his mistress?"

"All I know is he took good care of the kids in here. The rest of it, why should I care?"

When the skipping turns sporadic, the rhythm falling into an irregular beat, Ray Frey yells, "Done!" and the boys stop. Limp and boneless, several hit the floor. Others yank off sweat suits like they're on fire.

"Why was Mr. Holmes burying these people?"

"I told you—"

"Mr. Ray, Mr. Ray!"

Ray Frey's head swivels to a boy pointing at the floor. The old man darts—surprisingly agile—and kneels over the body sprawled across the linoleum. Vomit leaks from the parched lips.

"Call 911!" He scoops one hand behind the boy's neck. "Get me those ice packs!"

Four boys run to the back of the gym while others strip clothing from the unconscious boy, down to his underwear. I turn away, ashamed of staring at his near

200

nakedness. The boy's jogging suit, flung from their circle of concern, lands in front of me. It's nylon. Dark blue nylon.

"Mel!" Ray Frey hollers. "Wake up!"

Glancing over my shoulder, I watch Ray Frey slap the boy's cheeks. Suddenly, I recognize him—the small boxer who took a beating in the ring. Scratches and bruises cover the boy's ribcage, and a gash cuts his forehead. The last time I was here, Mel wore a T-shirt and head-gear, though the other boys were shirtless. Even when he left the ring, he didn't remove the headgear. I watch Ray Frey roll him sideways and scrape vomit from his mouth. I see another wound on Mel's right shoulder, the dark skin abraded to raw pink.

In the distance, sirens wail down Broad Street, an ambulance racing from the Medical College of Virginia. Ray Frey holds ice packs against Mel's neck and mumbles under his breath, his old face drawn with concern. The boys form a tight circle, hands on knobby knees.

I move slowly, reaching down, carefully folding each piece of Mel's sweat suit. I am a woman cleaning up this mess. That's all. And when the medics burst through the door, I shove his clothing into my purse and walk outside.

37

Three hours later, I'm searching the streets of DC for a parking spot that won't get the Benz towed. Since Phaup confiscated my ID, I can't access the Bureau's employee parking. I wind up walking all the way from G Street, feeling like a salmon swimming upstream. It's 5:30 p.m. on Friday, and everybody wants out of the city. I'm praying Mike Rodriguez isn't among them.

The guard at the public entrance checks my driver's license, then calls Hairs and Fibers for Mike. My purse goes through the X-ray machine, and I wait next to a wall of staff photographs memorializing FBI agents who died in the line of duty. I keep my back to the door, hoping nobody recognizes me. When Mike appears, his white lab coat is unbuttoned, his face flushed. "You forget your ID?" He vouches for me with the guard, signs the admittance form, and heads for the stairs.

"Let's go outside," I tell him.

He looks at me quizzically but follows me to the sidewalk teeming with people. Cabs stuck in traffic honk their horns. Buses belch black smoke.

"Raleigh, what's going on?"

I could lie, then pray for forgiveness. I could pretend I forgot my ID. I could make up some elaborate story that serves my purposes, and maybe in the end it would justify the means. And maybe not. What I know for certain is that very soon Phaup will close this case through John, and the truth will never be known. My city will continue to burn.

"Do you remember why you took this job?" I ask.

"Yeah, I had massive student loans."

Not the answer I was looking for. "Okay, but after the loans were paid off, why did you stay?"

"I guess because the job matters." He squints. "My work makes a difference."

"Right. That's my reason too." I tell him about my suspension, that I can't go upstairs because my ID has been confiscated for two weeks, that my supervisor is at this moment contacting the Office of Professional Responsibility.

"You're kidding me, right?" he asks.

"I need a favor, Mike. But I don't want to put you in a compromising situation."

"You already have."

Behind me, a cabbie leans on his horn. "You're right." I back away. "I shouldn't have come here."

"And now OPR is going to pay me a visit too because I just signed for you at the front desk."

I keep moving. "I'm sorry, I'm not thinking clearly."

He opens his mouth as three agents muscle through the revolving door, stepping out of separate compartments, adjusting sport coats over their shoulder holsters and moving down the sidewalk in a phalanx. They rubberneck a pretty woman walking past who is cursing because the cabs ignore her signal for a ride.

Mike walks toward me, pointing his finger. "When you went to Quantico, every one of us lab rats said you'd make a great agent."

"Okay, I'm sorry. You can stop. I'm leaving."

He grabs my arm. "My instincts tell me the suspension is wrong."

I look into his blue eyes. They're bedrock hard but clear.

"If OPR comes to me, I won't lie," he says. "But you've never been a glory hog, and this is obviously important to you."

I hand him the material rolled up in my purse, explaining the sweat suit should be compared with the nylon fibers recovered from the brick building. "I'm in no position to ask you to hurry."

"You're in no position to ask for anything," he says. "I'll call you in about an hour."

"Hey, Mike, thanks—"

"I'm not hurrying for you," he says. "The sooner this thing's outta here, the better."

———

Just past the Pentagon, as the Benz takes the exit for I-95 south, my cell phone rings.

Mike says, "You got yourself a match."

"You're sure?"

"After all this, you're questioning?"

I apologize.

"This fabric's specific nylon. Rip stop, water repellent,

and manufactured in Southeast Asia. They discontinued making it three years ago. I could do more extensive tests if I knew you weren't going to jail. But I did see the threading on the right shoulder, heavily abraded. A cursory evaluation says the material in the thread is probably brick. Red, coarse. I scraped what I could and put it on Eric's desk. He'll compare it with your brick samples."

"Oh no."

"Oh yes. I'm widening the circle of doom, Raleigh. When OPR comes around, I won't be the only sucker."

———

As always, I swing onto Route 1 as soon as possible for the drive south. Tonight, I also turn left into King's Charter, where Janine Falcon watches television with her son. That big purple creature named Barney is on the tube, singing about hand washing. The Falcon boy moves his chubby body side to side with the music, elbows tucked into his ribs just like the dinosaur.

"I was getting M.J. ready for bed," she says. "Do you mind waiting?"

She lays a soft blue blanket on the living room carpet. With one fluid motion, she pulls off the boy's shirt, barely interrupting his view of Barney. His skin is pale as moonstone, skin so new the vulnerability makes my heart ache. I take a seat on the couch and watch the dinosaurish thing bounce across the screen in his foam costume. Barney is the color of arsenic, and probably just as deadly to the nervous system.

"Did you find anything in that file?" Janine Falcon asks.

205

I turn to answer. The boy stands, wearing nothing. I want to look away. But not wanting to seem rude, I hold eye contact with the mother, explaining how some rather large pieces are missing from the puzzle. She listens as she pulls the pajama top over the boy's head—pajamas with Barney's image on them. Pointing at his shirt, he says, "Barr-neee!"

"That's right!" She claps her hands. "Barney! Very good!"

Suddenly, her face mixes emotions, joy and sorrow and the knowledge she can't share this amazing feat with her husband. I look away, back at the television, where the fake dinosaur walks in a disturbing manner, like a fat man with hemorrhoids. Barney admonishes the children to keep germs off their hands. "Always wash your hands before you eat," he tells them. "Always wash after using the restroom."

"Would you look at this?" she says.

My experience with new parents is that they find every single thing about their children interesting—including scatological details most adults would never discuss outside the doctor's office. With a sense of foreboding, I turn. The boy is on his back, tender feet in the air. He cranes his neck, keeping an eye on Barney. But his bare bottom is front and center, the skin enflamed with diaper rash.

"That's quite a rash," I say politely.

Barney says he loves me, that I love him, that we're one big happy family. Maybe this is why the boy likes the program.

"What I was wondering about were these things," she says.

I don't want to. But I have to. She's still holding his ankles with one hand, and with the other she wipes his blistered bottom with a disposable cloth. Scooting over to me, she says, "Look at this stuff. What are those things?" The wipe is right under my face, but it takes me a moment. Hundreds, no thousands of gelatinous beads the size of coarse sand roll across the white cloth. "Every time I take off M.J.'s diaper," she says, "I find these things all over his bottom. I wipe and wipe, and I still can't get them all off. Here he's got this horrible rash, and the pediatrician says—"

The used diaper sits on the edge of the blanket, a bloated paper clamshell. I walk over, pick it up. It's heavy, holding copious amounts of the boy's water. And yet, my palm is dry. With a disposable cloth, I brush the diaper's interior, uncovering another thousand gelatinous beads. I watch the mother tape a clean diaper around his bottom, a fresh diaper that lies flat as my notebook.

I hold up the dirty diaper. "Can I take this with me?"

Her smile softens dark smudges beneath her eyes. She is pretty once again. "Hey, I got a whole trash can full," she says. "You want those too?"

38

In the dark, Weyanoke's front lawn stretches like black slate to the river. Jillian answers the doorbell, her lovely face revealing her surprise. "Raleigh . . . are you . . . are you okay?"

"Is your father home?"

We walk down the dimly lighted gallery, Jillian glancing twice over her shoulder to survey my expression. In the sunroom, Mac, DeMott, and Harrison Fielding are playing cards on a leather-topped table. The scene stops me. Once again time stands still in the manor house, as the plantation family enjoys a summer evening of bridge while outside the world wages battle.

DeMott stands. "Raleigh, what's wrong?"

Harrison Fielding's peaty eyes fill with knowledge. Sighing, he fans his cards across the supple leather. "Too bad," he says wearily. "That was a good hand."

"Daddy?" Mac's voice quavers.

His eyes are bloodshot, either from the drink resting on the monogrammed coaster beside him, or another long day in some thoroughbred's saddle. "We were just enjoying a nice evening, Raleigh, when you arrive at our home without calling."

I push back every trained instinct, all those well-bred Virginia manners that would have me reflexively apologize for my sudden appearance. Instead, I think about Janine Falcon's family evening, putting her son to bed with a fake dinosaur for comfort. "How long was Detective Falcon providing security for your landfill?"

He frowns, a man dealing with a petulant child. "My landfill? That's why you're here?"

When I don't bite his stall for time, he continues.

"Perhaps I should have explained the security arrangement to you," he says. "It's true, Detective Falcon watched over my properties. But only when he was not on city payroll. As you'll recall, Raleigh, he died on patrol. Naturally, I was concerned for his widow. But perhaps you are not."

I'm still not biting. "He watched over the landfill. Is that correct?"

The muscular forearms stretch, gathering cards from the table. "Forgive me, Raleigh, but your investigation concerns possible civil rights violations committed by the detective on the factory roof. The factory, remember? The landfill is beyond your boundary."

"It's a federal crime to lie to an FBI agent."

"Daddy," Mac says. "What is going on here!"

"I want access to the landfill," I tell him. "If you choose not to cooperate, the United States Attorney's Office will get a court order."

"My landfill has nothing to do with this."

"U.S. Attorney it is." I turn to leave.

Jillian steps forward, taking my arm. "Daddy, for heaven's sake. This is Raleigh, she's our *friend*. Let's listen to her."

"She's an FBI agent." Mac slides behind her father. "She's probably recording our every word."

DeMott rolls his eyes. "Grow up, Mac."

She wraps lithe arms around her father, hugging him. "Make her stop."

"Sugar, that's not up to me. That's up to our . . . guest."

"When I was in custody, Dad, what did you say?" DeMott demands. "You said, 'Tell them everything.' Your exact words. Don't be a hypocrite."

The sudden guffaw startles everyone. Peery Fielding is standing in the doorway, her ample curves swaddled in peach silk. She floats into the room. The skin on her face looks tight as a drum. "DeMott, your father maintains standards that do not apply to him. Harrison Fielding simply decides for everyone else." She extends her hand, taking mine. "Raleigh, nice to see you. I would have preferred different circumstances, but once again life ignores my wishes." When she turns toward her husband, she is still holding my hand. The gesture is both comforting and disturbing. "Harrison, tell Raleigh what she needs to know."

He glowers at her. "My dear wife enjoys ultimatums."

"So does the FBI," I tell him.

Peery gives my hand a squeeze. "Oh, I do so like this girl!"

Picking up his drink, Harrison Fielding rattles the ice. "Lawyers tend to complicate the obvious. We don't need to involve them."

My relief is huge, yet concealed. Whatever card game Fielding was playing tonight, I played poker with a great bluff. I'm in no position to get the U.S. Attorneys involved; even Charlie Reynolds couldn't help me now. Peery gives my hand another squeeze, then walks me to the front door.

Behind us, Harrison Fielding calls out my name. I still haven't told him why I need to see the landfill. But I've broken every other etiquette rule tonight, so I leave Weyanoke without replying. And Peery Fielding smiles.

39

From the carriage house, I can see my mother weeding the garden in her new straw hat. With a serrated bread knife, she decapitates dandelions invading the slate patio then tosses the yellow carcasses over her shoulder. Behind her, Madame snoozes on the warm stone. I shower, dress, and walk down to the courtyard, asking to borrow the Benz. Again. I tell her my car is still in the shop.

I'm getting too comfortable lying.

———

The City Hall records office is on the eleventh floor and is controlled by a taciturn clerk who logs me into a public computer and walks away. Twenty minutes later I've found the records on the P Street landfill. The proposal for dumping and storing garbage in a residential neighborhood provoked thirteen complaints. All anonymous. The complaints cite "potential problems with stench, contamination, rodents, and commercial traffic." But at the public hearing, nobody came forward to testify against Weyanoke Enterprises. The company spokesperson reminded the council that "the waste management corporation" had filed "all necessary permits with the city, state, and the EPA." The landfill, he noted, would provide the city with abundant tax revenue.

Two weeks later, my government at work, Richmond city council approved the P Street Garbage Receptacle. The waste will be buried with the highly acidic dirt scraped from the bluff. Scrolling to the bottom, I check the vote: 8 to 1. The last time Richmond city council voted 8 to 1 was to erect a statue of Arthur Ashe, the late tennis star who grew up on Richmond's segregated courts.

Other than trash and tennis, Richmond can't agree about anything.

In this case, the landfill's lone dissenter was Morton Thalbrough. I glance at the city map hanging behind the clerk's desk. Council member names aren't listed on the districts, because the seats come up for reelection every two years. "Excuse me," I ask the clerk. "Which district does Morton Thalbrough represent?"

She looks up. "The West End."

But the landfill is not located in the West End, the wealthiest part of town. I walk over to her desk. From a cartography standpoint, it's a good map, heavily detailed with streets and natural barriers. I can see where Main Street turns into Williamsburg Road, how the road follows the geologic contours through Fulton Hill at P Street then abruptly ends. That would be the bluff, deemed safe for garbage burial.

The district is marked with a blue number 6.

"So Thalbrough has the First," I say. "Who runs the Sixth District?"

213

She smiles. "You're not from Richmond, are you?"

"Why would you say that?"

"Everybody knows who runs the Sixth."

"I don't."

"The Sixth belongs to LuLu Mendant." She points to the map. "Right there, that's LuLu Country."

———

LuLu Mendant, five-term councilman and current mayor of Richmond, is not in his office on the second floor, but I leave my card with a bored receptionist answering Saturday phone calls for the mayor. I take the escalator to the lobby, passing that ghastly statue attempting to stop violence in our community, and step outside to Broad Street. A mass of overheated humanity swarms the bus stop. In my bag I find LuLu Mendant's business card—"Esq." is embossed in gold after his name—and call his law office. Mr. Mendant is out for the day, his other receptionist assures me, but he will be in touch as soon as possible. His people work Saturdays; he doesn't.

I hang up, squinting into the sun. A young woman walks by wearing a child on her back. The boy is hoisted by a backpack, lifting and lowering his arms in rhythm with his mother's steps. As they pass, I hear his singing, his bell-like voice lilting on the summer air.

40

On the east side of Church Hill, a dog barks. It's a hoarse, monotonous warning from an animal that sees constant predators. I listen to the barks as two cars drive down P Street. The first is a black BMW, followed by DeMott's rattletrap Ford truck.

Harrison Fielding parks the Beemer two feet from the curb, careful to keep his wheels off the broken glass that sprays across the pavement like petrified tears.

It is 7:00 p.m. The landfill is closed for the day.

Flicking keys from a leather holder, Mr. Fielding pops the chambers on three massive Schlage padlocks. "DeMott," he says.

Shouldering the gate, DeMott pulls the heavy chains and lifts the fencing so it chatters across pebbly concrete hastily poured because the landfill went in so fast. Just inside the gate, a wooden shack is painted flame orange. Four windows, one on each side, look over the mountain of garbage piled against a seventy-five-foot bluff. Behind us, an old cargo van arrives, making a difficult turn around the Beemer. A large black man climbs out and lumbers over.

"This is Al Gibson," Mr. Fielding says without looking at me. "Al manages the landfill. Al, this is the FBI agent I told you about."

Al Gibson shakes my hand, his palm like riprap rock.

"Do you keep track of your deliveries?" I ask.

"I got everything in a log book, in the shack," he says, glancing at his boss.

"If the gate was closed, how would I get in?" I ask.

"You wouldn't," Mr. Fielding snaps. "We keep the gate locked, you might have noticed. Nobody gets in or out."

"There's always a way in, even if the gate's locked," I say. "What about the top of that bluff, is there a trail down?"

"There's some homeless folks on top of the bluff," Al Gibson says. "Sometimes they come down the hill. I called the police about it."

I glance at Mr. Fielding.

"I have better things to do with my time," he says, striding toward the black car, driving away.

———

I stare at the top of the bluff. The soil is taupe-colored, void of grass and weeds, and as the bluff descends the dirt turns grayish-green. In the hot evening air, the garbage's sickly sweet smell turns my stomach. Sooty seagulls camp on the waste heaps, picking open trash bags, screeching at one another. Al Gibson waits in the orange shack while I walk to Wally's apple green Duster—no way would I bring the Benz up here—with a trunk almost rusted through. My equipment is in Rubbermaid bins too big to fall through the holes. I take out some film canisters,

216

stuffing them in my hip pack, then strap the Nikon around my shoulder.

"What do you want me to do?" DeMott has followed me to the car.

"Nothing."

"Don't be like that, Raleigh."

"It's not personal." I'm already skating thin ice, being here under suspension. He'll only make things worse. "If you do anything significant, the investigation is compromised."

"Investigation?"

The sign on the orange shack reads "Wipe Your Feet." Al Gibson sits on a stool inside, looking out the north window at the garbage, at the filthy scavenging birds. I'll tell him I'm going to walk around for a while; he says he'll wait for me here.

"You can go now, I'm fine," I tell DeMott.

"That's all right." He shrugs. "I'll just hang around in case you need something."

"Your father told you to stick to me?"

He nods. "Like glue."

41

The seagulls gust up hot air. They hover above my head, dirty gray birds with faces pointed as arrows. Suddenly, they plunge like bullets fired from invisible chambers. The sun blinds me, and I raise a hand, shielding my eyes. Someone knocks behind me. It's a man in the orange shack, the man is not Al Gibson. He is white. And he is somehow familiar.

Pointing to the sky, the man mouths one word.

Look, he says. *Look.*

I step toward him, trying to get a better view. His face . . .

"Dad? Dad, what are you doing here?"

He points at the sky again. *Raleigh, look at the birds!*

I turn around. The seagulls swarm the garbage, needling sharp beaks into the plastic bags, savagely flinging the contents. Then one by one, the birds fly away, and the sun drops behind the bluff. I can see the birds clearly now. See the things clutched in their greedy beaks, gripped tightly with their filthy talons.

Things I do not want to see.

I turn around, but my father continues to point at the sky. *Look.*

The birds circle, turning an endless loop against the lapis sky. One bird follows the next until they form a perfect figure eight, the symbol for infinity.

"Raleigh."

I turn around. The shack is empty. "Dad?"

"Raleigh Ann."

"Dad?"

I turn my own circle, searching, trying to find him. But all I see is the garbage, the peculiar green soil, the infinity of birds over my head.

"Wake up, Raleigh."

I open my eyes. My mother is leaning over me. Her long necklace dangles in my face. "Sugarplum," she says, "napping is one of the things that ruin circadian rhythms."

I glance around the room, disoriented. My heart pounds. I try to remember what happened: I came in the house, found no one, turned on the television, lay down on the couch. Now a gardening show host explains composting. I push myself up. Madame trots over then licks my palm.

"Wally wanted more pictures of the camp," my mother says. "We heard a man from the Philippines. A missionary."

"Oh. Good."

"Wally said let you sleep. He says you've been working overtime. But I told him, 'A little sleep, a little slumber, and poverty comes on you like a bandit.' He just rolled his eyes and said he already got his daily allowance of Scripture, thank you very much." She fiddles with the necklace. "Raleigh, are you feeling all right?"

"I'm fine. What time is it?"

"Nearly nine o'clock." Her blouse is the color of lava. Her skirt cuts three inches above the knee. The Pentecostals must have loved that. "I know what you need," she says. "Protein. All this running around collecting rocks, your system is begging for amino acids." She walks into the kitchen, Madame follows, and I stare blankly at the gardening show, where a man resembling an elf extols the virtues of nitrogen and the processes of decomposition. I walk into the kitchen. She stands at the stove, poking a slab of tofu with a spatula.

"Do you ever dream about Dad?" I ask.

She grips the garlic press with both hands, crushing one clove. Then under her breath says, "Oh, why not, she's not dating," as she throws three more cloves into the pan. The sizzle fills the room with a sharp salty scent.

"Mom?"

"He had red hair."

"Excuse me?"

"In my last dream, your father had red hair. It was so strange. He never had red hair. Not even as a child. At first, I thought maybe it wasn't him. You know that happens. People pretend to be someone you love just to convince you to do things you would not otherwise do. You have to be very careful." She turns around, her hazel eyes troubled. "Do you understand?"

"I understand Dad had red hair in your dream."

220

"Red, yes. I wondered about that. Then I decided: fire."

"Fire?"

"Red is the color of fire. Your father was warning me we're going to have a fire. And then we had that lamp blow up in the den, remember?"

"You dreamed Dad had red hair. That's all."

She shoves the tofu with the spatula.

"So," I say cheerfully, "tell me about your day."

"The doors don't open."

"What doors?"

"At the camp. Some doors don't open. The sign says 'Alarm Will Sound.'"

"Those would be fire exits." But she must know that. Doesn't she?

"Alarm Will Sound. Isn't that a strange phrase," she says. "The words move forward and backward at the same time. 'Alarm will sound' or 'Sound will alarm.' And either way it's right, depending on which way you go through the door. Look in the refrigerator, there's some rice from last night."

I open the refrigerator, feeling a familiar dread creep across my heart. The high manic spill of words, the strange look in her eyes. And the guilt I feel for asking about my father. *Heal her. Please, heal her.*

"Did you find it?" she asks. "Look for a glass bowl. I never use plastic because it leaches hormones into the food. You should remember that."

I place the bowl on the counter. "I'll be right back."

In the living room, I stare out the window at the night, trying to see the sky. But the lights around Robert E. Lee glow too brightly tonight. Some guys are playing Frisbee on the dark apron of grass, their movements stroboscopic as they pass in and out of the general's floodlights.

"What's wrong?" Wally has one hand on the staircase balustrade, his skin nearly as dark as the walnut wood.

"Nothing."

"Nadine."

I nod. "Did she tell you about the fire exits?"

"The forward-backward thing? Yeah, she mentioned it on the ride home. But I smell garlic, so she didn't crack up completely."

I stare out the window.

"Hey, it's a joke," he says.

"I wish I felt like laughing."

42

Later that night, standing outside John Breit's condominium building on Stafford Street, I can smell garlic on my breath. The apartment building is one of the Fan's many converted residences, wedged between two narrow alleys. On the phone box bolted beside the entrance, I dial his apartment. He buzzes me in, and turquoise carpet leads to apartment #10.

John's watching a baseball game while sitting in an emerald green leather chair, that monstrous style of furniture men love and women despise. "These Braves," he tells me. "Worst thing for my blood pressure."

The only other chair is a yellow velour number, the arms stained black. I sit.

"You want a beer?" he asks.

"No, thanks. I don't drink."

"I forgot." He pauses. "Actually, I didn't forget. But since you're suspended, I thought maybe you'd changed your ways." He gets up and walks to the kitchen, which is just paces away. The back of his polo shirt is wrinkled from a night of beer and baseball in the big chair.

"Did you hear about it from Phaup?" I ask.

"I would have guessed the same thing," he says over his shoulder. "I was surprised when she didn't make an example of you. But she got called out of town, so she just didn't get the chance."

"How did you find out?"

"Raleigh, it's an office of trained investigators." He walks back, holding the brown beer bottle by the neck, and plunks back into the chair. "Already there's a betting pool on why you got yanked. White Collar says you messed up your paperwork—typical, everything's paper with those guys. But considering Phaup's need for bureaucracy, that's not a bad guess. Meanwhile, Sex Crimes says you're traumatized by the guys who attacked you down at the river."

So they know about that too. Fantastic. "What was your bet?"

He rubs his jaw, scratching the five o'clock shadow. "You're young, idealistic to a fault. It ticks off Phaup. The way I see it, there's the problem, you and Phaup. By the way, she gave me your 44 before she left."

"And you still managed to figure out I was suspended? Gosh, you really are a trained investigator."

"Every once in a while, I have to do some hard thinking." He grins. "So, you came to tell me about the suspension, but we got that out of the way. Stay for the game. It's not like you have to get up early tomorrow."

"Thanks."

"Hey, Raleigh, it happens. Way back, I drank a beer with lunch and got suspended for thirty days. *Thirty days.* Imagine what that did for my marriage."

"Why were you drinking at lunch?" At Quantico,

224

they told us the legal drinking age for agents was fifty-seven, the Bureau's mandatory retirement age for agents.

John acts like this is the dumbest question a trained investigator could ask. "When I signed on, drinking wasn't a big deal. Nobody got bombed, at least not on duty. We had a couple beers with lunch, met at bars after work. And if we had a long road trip and nothing in between, we loaded up the cooler and enjoyed the ride."

"You sound wistful."

"We were better agents back then. We met people, found good sources." He turns back to the baseball game. "Never mind. It's not worth moaning about. I'm retiring in two months."

The Braves pitcher walks two Orioles, and the commentators slip into the blather of vastly uneven games—chitchat about player superstitions, things their Little League coaches told them. John lets out a sigh. "You're dying to tell me about the 44. Aren't you?"

I nod.

"Game's over anyway." He clicks the remote and sets his beer on the coffee table strewn with water rings.

I tell him about Detective Falcon's "ghost"—the cold case he wanted to solve and couldn't. How Holmes paid for the girl's funeral and made a family with her sister.

"He was a busy guy."

"Holmes buried people he didn't know. And they're all cold cases. Every one's an unsolved murder. The detective's partner checked the files for me. Most of them were shot with a .38, execution style. Or beaten to death."

John shakes his head. "Raleigh, this is a civil rights case."

I explain that fibers from the brick don't match clothing from Holmes or Detective Falcon. "But they match a nylon sweat suit from a kid at the boxing gym. That kid was on the roof that Saturday." I explain the shoe soil, full of the acrylamide that's rampant in landfills because of disposable diapers. "Both of those men went into that landfill before they met on the roof. Why?"

John finishes his beer. "You sent clothing samples to the lab *after* you were suspended?"

I don't bother defending myself because he won't like what I say next, either. "I had a dream tonight." I describe the birds, the garbage, what the seagulls carried away. "They were carrying body parts."

"And your dad told you to look at that?" He walks into the kitchen. I hear another *pfft* of a beer opening. "And now you're going to tell me why he wanted you to see that."

"There's a body in that landfill."

He downs half the bottle before looking at me. I feel the Senior Agent Lecture about to begin.

"Raleigh, you stuck to this case even when Phaup took you out," he says. "That speaks volumes about what kind of agent you are. I'm proud of you, in that sense."

"But."

"But you gotta let go. It's a 44. What did I tell you, that first day on Southside? Civil rights goes nowhere. And right now you are more than nowhere. You're suspended."

And he's a fifty-six-year-old man who looks seventy.

Two divorces, two kids who won't speak to him, a one-bedroom condo with the square footage of a kennel. But I know he called in that pink bicycle our first day out. Somewhere deep inside, his heart beats. And it beats for justice.

"Okay," I tell him. "From now on I'll only work the easy cases. And while I'm at it, I'll call the Richmond PD and tell them to forget about what happened to my dad in that alley. If his case is too hard to figure out, don't even worry about it."

"That's not what I meant."

"Then help me, John. Help me figure this out."

He sighs, shaking his head. "And if we find nothing, you'll leave me alone. I close the case. End of story?"

"Yes. End of story."

43

When John arrives at the landfill the following morning, he's groggy. At least until the sun starts warming the garbage. He's wide awake when the backhoe stirs the stench and the metal basket swinging twenty feet above us drips landfill juices.

"You owe me so big for this," he says.

I watch the metal basket graze the sky, releasing its ugly confetti. Torn plastic jugs. Oily paper bags. Coffee grounds. Moldy cold cuts. Juice cartons. And dirty diapers, diapers, diapers. Even with a bandana tied over my nose and mouth, the smell keeps my gag reflex constant. We reach into the piles, John and I both wearing heavy black latex gloves.

I tear open a Hefty bag. My throat convulses. "What is that?"

John plunges his right glove into the brown mush. He doesn't seem to share the same revulsion. But then I guarantee his refrigerator contains furry specimens that once were food. "Ground beef." He holds a handful for my inspection. Yellow maggots crawl through the meat.

"You're sure?"

"See the plastic tray?" He kicks it with his tennis shoe, then drops the wormy beef. His T-shirt reads: "Pull Up Your Shorts." "Raleigh, you realize if all we find is hamburger, you're the one who's dead meat."

The backhoe swings overhead, taking trash from the main heap and depositing it at the far end of the bluff so John and I can paw through it. The odor is unbelievably foul. My skin feels prickly from the heat, sticky with airborne particulate. An hour later, I can tell John's having those nasty second thoughts, the ones that obliterate good first thoughts.

I'm having them myself. We start going over how he can cover his tracks.

"I'm already suspended," I tell him.

"Nobody told me anything," he insists. "They ask, you were concerned about some landfill connection to the detective. And since Phaup was out of town I couldn't ask her permission. She never told me you were suspended. You lied to me."

"Okay."

"I can retire faster than they can fire me."

"Okay."

Using Al Gibson's log books, I sketched a rough stratigraphy of the garbage this morning. Lighter loads arrive Tuesdays and Wednesdays, heavier deposits before and after the weekends. Judging by my conversation with Mrs. Saunders, the mother of the dead girl in the cold case file, her second daughter disappeared right before the roof fall. That's more than two weeks ago, and two weeks of waste is an enormous amount of garbage. We've already gone through twenty-five feet of the pile, and only five feet remain, a soupy mixture of now unrecognizable objects. All that is discernable are the fat maggots and waterproof diapers that seem indestructible.

"Maybe we should slow down," I say. "It's hard to tell what anything is anymore."

John looks over at me. His right hand holds a clump of paper, and he peels away the wet gray pulp. It's a sandal. A woman's sandal, the kind my mother would wear, the four-inch heel tapering to lethal punctuation. The sparkly blue strap is torn, but a silver buckle no bigger than a dime holds fast.

"What do you think?" John says.

"Look at the strap," I tell him. "Somebody tossed it because it's broken."

"Women don't fix these shoes?"

I wouldn't know; I don't wear shoes like that. But my mother would probably throw it out. "Cheaper to toss it."

"Well, bag it anyway. I might need something to explain this later."

I carry the dripping sandal to John's Cadillac, which he backed into a dry area far from the dump and the orange shack, before extracting an ironclad promise from me not to open any of the car's doors. Only the trunk. "It took thirty-two years to get a car like this, Raleigh. I don't want it smelling like puke now." I drop the sandal into a clear evidence bag, mark time, date, and location, then seal it with evidence tape. I seal it twice, just in case anything leaks and I further annoy

230

John, who is doing me a favor so big I will never be able to repay him.

"What was that?" Al Gibson stares at the plastic bag containing the sandal.

Nothing, I tell him.

"Raleigh!" John yells. "Get over here!"

His right arm is stretched out from his body, the glove dripping juices. He doesn't want me chatting while he's up to his ankles in landfill juice. I drop the evidence bag into the trunk, then wait for the Cadillac's excruciatingly slow mechanism to close. I've been repeatedly instructed not to push on the trunk. When I hear it click, I jog back to John and the garbage piles. The air smells like something from the lower rung of hell.

John points.

I see more garbage swimming in acidic juices—a torn plastic baggy protecting a moldy sandwich, one tricycle with mangled front wheels, wet coffee filters weaving the spokes.

I squat down.

The skin is green with bloat, but the foot's toenails shine from the black trash bag. Taking a pen from my pocket, I brush maggots off the skin. Red nail polish sparkles in the sunlight, a pedicure defiant of all the rot surrounding it. I scatter more maggots from the toes, the larvae quivering as they fall.

———◆———

At the Jeff Davis Apartments, the grandchildren are inside, protected from the fierce heat. Mrs. Saunders takes one look at me and tells them, "Go turn on the TV in Granny's bedroom."

She lights her cigarette, and I begin slowly, keeping my voice low so it can't be heard over the television in the other room. She listens, then exhales smoke. "Cherry's not coming home. That's what you come to tell me."

"We need to run some tests, for identification." I ask about a dentist, and she says the family goes to MCV, where dental students treat them for free. When I ask to borrow a comb or toothbrush belonging to her daughter, she turns automatically, returning with a comb containing dark hair fragments. I take an evidence bag from my purse, and she drops the comb inside.

Pressing her lips together, she controls the quiver in her chin. "What'd they do to her?"

"We still don't know it's her."

I ask where her daughter got her nails done. Mrs. Saunders holds her hand up, displaying the pink nails. Suddenly, I place the acrid odor in the apartment, the chemical bite hanging in the air. Acetone. Nail polish remover. And the hall closet reveals her supplies—polish, sets of acrylic nails, white cotton balls, big bottles of acetone. "This here," she says, handing me a bottle of red polish, "this is her color. It's called 'Cherry Dreams.' She wouldn't use nothing else."

I open another evidence bag. She drops it in.

44

Among the most jarring sights on earth is a dead body naked under fluorescent light.

The body bag is gone, and the maggots lay dead on the stainless steel gurney, sprayed with insecticide by the morgue's lab assistants, who have also washed the body and placed the foot beside the leg like a doll's broken limb.

Goose bumps erupt on my arms, and I rub my skin.

"Cold?" John asks.

I nod. The temperature hovers at fifty degrees. Surgical scrubs cover our shoes and clothing, cotton masks cover our faces. But the masks don't alleviate the stench. Not as overwhelming as the landfill but more insidious. Sharp, playing on the imagination. The temperature isn't the only thing that chills me.

I've been to the morgue too many times; it's a place that strikes me as some terrible way station of death. Neither here nor there, the bodies lie stiff, motionless on stainless steel gurneys like cold hard facts reminding you how every heartbeat will stop, sometimes violently. Each time I come here it's because somebody has lived their life in a sustained rage against God or because they became the target of that rage. Murder. Mutilation. Deadly assault. Mothers. Fathers. Sons. Daughters.

"I hate this smell more than that garbage dump," John says.

I nod.

He wonders aloud how long it would take the state lab to match the DNA, if we can't get dental records. How maybe we should send the comb to the DC lab, even though it'll enrage Phaup, because what does he care? By the time Phaup files the paperwork against him, he'll be retired. He keeps talking until the swinging metal doors open. Richmond's chief medical examiner bursts into the room.

Yardley Bauer is petite, blond, midforties. I've never worked an autopsy with her, but her personality seems on par with the room's stainless steel. Maybe it's an occupational hazard.

Bauer reads the clipboard. "How deep in the landfill was it?"

John turns to me. "What, thirty feet?"

"Nobody got the exact depth?" she growls.

"Agent Harmon?" John smiles at me in a weird way.

"I did a rough stratigraphic record of the landfill, based on delivery averages." I clear my throat; it's been awhile since I spoke. "The victim was discovered near the bottom of the pile, placing her among deliveries approximately seventeen days old."

John grins at Bauer, Bauer ignores him.

"I doubt the body was there that long," she says dismissively. "Was the foot with it?"

234

"We found that first," John says. "It might've happened from the backhoe. Actually, we found a sandal first. Really, really high heel." His eyebrows move up and down, he's almost leering.

Bauer snaps on a pair of latex gloves then cradles the rotting foot. "I see signs of violent amputation. The sheer weight of all that garbage could break bone, particularly if the body was suffering rigor. Decomposition severed the skin." She writes something on the clipboard and returns to the body. "Gunshot wound, back of the head. Probable cause of death."

She lifts an electric saw and cuts into the skull. I turn around, staring at a steel counter across the room. When finally the buzzing stops, I turn around. Bauer holds a bullet in her bloody fingers. "Looks like a .38." She casually tosses it into a metal pan.

"We found the body wrapped in plastic," John says. "So we didn't see any head wound."

"What kind of plastic?"

"Lawn bags," he tells her. "They were duct-taped around the body like a mummy."

"Well, that explains the preservation. I take back what I said about how long the body was in the landfill." With the summer heat, Bauer says, the body would have decomposed quickly, and on a timetable that would accelerate with the acidic properties of refuse. Her small hand hovers two inches above the mottled green skin. Wisps of pale blond hair peek from under the cotton cap. Somehow, even with bloody fingers and an apron saturated with blood, Bauer looks sparkling

235

clean. She reminds me of a diamond—the earth's hardest substance. Her hand stops. "There."

"There, where?" John says.

Bauer points at the right leg, which has some black indentations in the skin. "See those?"

"Worms?" he says. "Yeah. I've been looking at them all day."

"Those are pupae sacs," I tell him.

For the first time, Bauer looks directly at me. "Yes, that's correct."

"Raleigh used to work in the bureau's forensic lab, in DC," John explains.

"Entymology?"

"Mineralogy."

"All right, Agent Harmon," she says. "Explain to him the significance of these 'worm' holes."

"Empty pupae cases are what's left behind when the maggots turn into flies. If you find pupae sacs, it means at least one fly cycle has taken place since time of death. Each fly cycle requires at least fourteen days."

She asks about my soil samples. "Tell Agent Breit why the soil's important." Bauer's eyes twinkle. She's enjoying the talk over his head, playing with his ego.

"As the human body decomposes, it releases five fatty acids," I explain. "The acids vary with time, so soil analysis can sometimes pinpoint time of death."

John looks at Bauer. "So what do we need you for?"

She throws him a withering glance. "My concern is that landfill seepage will interfere with fatty acid detection." She snaps off the gloves. "I'll call you when I'm ready for a full autopsy. In the meantime, I'll write up what I have."

236

"You have my number," John says.

We walk out, and I'm wondering what just happened. Why the examination was cut short. Why John acted so oddly, leering during an autopsy. On Jackson Street, the sidewalk radiates like a pizza oven. But a morgue chill penetrates my bones. I'm still shivering.

John lights a cigarette.

"You smoke?" I'm shocked.

"Only after being in there," he says. "It gets rid of that dead smell, you know."

I reach into my purse for a breath mint and find an evidence bag from Mrs. Saunders. John didn't think the polish would mean anything to the investigation.

"Cherry Dreams," I tell him. "Probably what's on her toes. I should take this back to the mother."

John exhales appreciatively. "You want them to check it?" It's his call now. But it does a suspended soul good that he asked.

"When does Phaup get back?"

"Two days," he says. "We have to hurry." The cigarette is already burned halfway, he's puffing it with every breath. "Run in, give it to her. I'll wait here."

Back in the medical examiner's building, I tell the receptionist I need to speak with Bauer again. When Bauer comes striding out of her office, she's in fresh scrubs. "Forget something?" She says this as though we're good friends now, science girls who speak the same foreign language.

I hold up the bottle of nail polish. "The pedicure; he wants to see if it matches this polish."

Her eyes are so light they're yellow citrine. After taking the bottle from my hand, she turns it slowly. "What mineral does this remind you of, Agent Harmon?"

"Corundum. The red form of corundum."

"Corundum wouldn't sell nail polish," she says. "But ruby red might."

Ruby—it's the red form of corundum. She's caught me showing off. It was probably her game plan.

She raises an eyebrow. "Is he outside smoking a ciga-rette?"

"Yes."

Her smile is feline. And I realize that John's craving for smoke has nothing to do with the stench of death. But it has everything to do with the way certain people pierce the human heart.

45

On East Franklin Street, a yellow school bus opens its pneumatic doors and sighs, releasing a thin black girl. The bus belongs to St. Catherine's School, my alma mater, and the girl skips across the street, her pleated uniform parachuting around thin legs. She bounds up a brick stoop and hops inside. The front door of the house is as yellow as the school bus.

I park, lock the car, and admire the view of the James River below. Nearly two hundred years ago, this spectacular vista drew tobacco traders and cotton merchants, the men who built these tall Georgians on Church Hill, houses that would testify to fortune. Of course, most of the fortunes owed some debt to the economic advantages of slavery, and most of the fortunes disappeared with the War of Northern Aggression. By 1950, when Brown vs. Board of Education started playing out in nearby Prince William County, Richmond's white exodus hit full speed. Over the next twenty years, squatters and scavengers and salvage yards hollowed out the proud Georgian homes.

But history does more than repeat itself; it pivots on

paradox. Today, the Church Hill houses have been refurbished right down to the handmade shutters and gas lanterns. But now the owners are black, many of them descendants of slaves, the inadvertent inheritors of antebellum fortunes.

Still, LuLu Mendant's three-story Georgian stands in defiant contrast to its tasteful neighbors. Crimson awnings hunch over the sash windows, the brick is painted azure blue, and, of course, the door is yellow. Dog droppings have turned the front yard to straw. When I knock on the front door, the presumed depositor barks his warning.

"Don't you people know how to call?" the mayor says.

"I was in the neighborhood."

He grunts disbelief. "The dog doesn't bite. Unless I tell him to."

As I suspected, the dog is a terrier, a true ankle-chewer. Madame would send him packing. I step into the foyer, and LuLu releases the dog. It scrambles across the polished marble floor and sniffs my pant leg furiously.

"If you still want names from the demonstration, it's not going to happen," he tells me. "Nobody saw anything."

"Well, that's that."

The mayor reaches for the brass doorknob, believing we're done. "Y'all better come to some conclusions soon. People don't like waiting like this."

The dog scurries to my other leg. "What can you tell me about the landfill over on P Street?" I ask.

He scowls, clouding his smoky agate eyes. "The landfill? What's that got to do with anything?"

240

"We found a body in there this morning."

"J.R.!" The dog ignores him.

"J.R.!" Still no response.

The mayor looks up the stairs. "Marlene! Get down here!"

The girl from the St. Catherine's school bus appears at the top of the stairs. "Take your dog," he says, and Marlene saunters down, slowly as possible, all teenage attitude, and scoops up the dog. J.R. stares at us contemptuously over her shoulder as LuLu escorts me into the parlor just off the foyer. He slides tall wooden pocket doors, enclosing the room with walls upholstered in amber suede. I take a seat on a red velvet fainting couch while LuLu, his back to me, shuffles cigars in a wooden humidor on a round teak table. Finally, he extracts what appears to be a scud missile. "The landfill," he says, "that's what you asked about?"

His rough voice sounds different, as though the suede walls absorb every syllable. In fact, the entire world feels shut out. I move my jaw back and forth, trying to pop my ears, waiting for him to light the cigar. Then I realize the room has no tobacco aroma. He's just going to hold it.

"Why did you support the landfill going in up here?" I ask.

"Why?" His tone of voice makes my question sound ridiculous. "In case you haven't noticed, this city needs money."

"Harrison Fielding owns that land."

"So?"

"So you pushed his landfill through the council but organized a protest against his hat factory."

241

"Hat factory? You make it sound like a legitimate business. That *factory* is nothing but empty space. Takes the whole city block, and the man doesn't pay taxes."

"So once the landfill was in, you could protest the factory. Is that the deal you two worked out?"

"I organized that protest on principle," he says, carefully not denying any deals with Fielding.

"What principle was that?"

"Reparations."

"For?"

"Slavery. What else is there? The black slave built that Fielding fortune, and it's time the family pays us for all that free work."

I know my Fielding history. So does LuLu Mendant. But I remind him the Fieldings sided with the North during the Civil War. "They voluntarily freed their slaves."

"They still had slaves."

I'm about to say something, then stop, admiring the politician's acumen. How easily he steered me off track. He's a master. "The FBI discovered a body in the landfill this morning," I say.

But the mayor doesn't even feign surprise. Twisting the cigar, he evaluates the luxurious brown wrap for several moments. "My constituents make sure I know everything here on the Hill."

"Maybe you know who she is too."

The agate eyes darken. "I called for a civil rights investigation. Y'all are supposed to find out how that white cop murdered a black man in broad daylight."

"Let's get back to Fielding," I say, not playing his game. "He never could have put in the landfill without your

242

support. He needed you, because he needed the black votes on council. The whites were already for it. But once you supported it, nobody could stop it. What did he offer you?"

He leans forward, shaking his head. "Take that fancy car you parked outside my house and drive around Church Hill. Ask these folks what they need. They'll tell you: They need money. Money for schools. Money to feed their families. Money because they can't find jobs."

"So you collected money from Fielding, for the city. How much did you get yourself?"

He stands up. "You got some nerve, coming in my house like this." He drops the cigar in the humidor and opens the pocket doors. Sound washes into the room. Suddenly, I can hear a monotonous murmur of hip-hop coming from upstairs. The sharp click of dog claws on the floor above us. The soft whoosh of an air-conditioning system blowing from the ceiling.

The mayor opens the front door without saying good-bye.

46

The mayor's locks tumble behind me. And in the distance, church bells ring.

I drive the Benz down East Franklin to the corner of 25th Street, and park. As I walk toward St. John's church, the bells stop ringing. But the parish cemetery seems to hold percussive echoes in the ancient gravestones. The mother of Edgar Allan Poe is buried here; so are some eighteenth-century Harmons, the people who helped build this Episcopal parish in what was then the frontier of the New World. Now a historic landmark, St. John's gets a steady stream of tourists. They come to see where Patrick Henry delivered his famous ultimatum for liberty or death in 1775. And as I slip into the cool dark sanctuary, a tour is already underway. The guide wears a plumy white shirt with knickers and describes Richmond on the eve of the Revolutionary War. I close the box pew door that belonged to centuries of Harmons. It squeaks loudly.

"Ma'am," the guide calls to me. "You are welcome to listen, but please turn off any electronic devices."

Privacy shattered, I'm even more upset about being

called *ma'am* instead of *miss*. Reaching into my bag, I turn off my cell phone and listen to the guide explain how the Second Continental Congress met here, how Thomas Jefferson and George Washington discussed the future of the colonies in this very room. And how, several years later, Benedict Arnold, the infamous traitor, prepared to take a defenseless Richmond by quartering British troops here.

The tourists gape around the sanctuary, then stare at me, a stranger lurking in a box pew instead of joining the tour. I bow my head, pretending to pray. When I was six years old, I attended my first service here, and my father had to explain the strange pews, why so tall with a swinging door on the aisle: early Revolutionary parishioners brought hot bricks to the unheated church services and the box pew retained the heat.

"As you can see," the guide says, "St. John's has an unusual ceiling."

And during my father's funeral, I stared at that concave plaster ceiling for the entire service, hoping that when I looked back, David Harmon would be alive. Sitting right here, holding his worn Bible in one hand, my mother's hand in the other.

"We will conclude our tour of St. John's with a reenactment of the Second Virginia Convention of 1775," the guide says. "This is more commonly known as the Patrick Henry reenactment. We ask that you please refrain from recording the speech." Bootlegs of Patrick Henry's speech, he explains, are popping up on the Internet. The church sells an official tape, with proceeds supporting historic preservation. I make a mental note, since bootlegging falls under Bureau jurisdiction, and watch as several performers walk into the sanctuary, each dressed in colonial clothing. Though I've heard the reenactment several times, it's worth hearing again. And again. Nothing puts your citizenship into perspective like Patrick Henry's speech.

"One more request," the guide adds. "Please don't cough."

The tourists laugh.

"I'm serious," he says. "We will be recording today's reenactment as part of my master's thesis in history." The audience applauds; the guide bows extravagantly. And because someone asks, the guide quickly explains how electricians wired the church for sound, running the lines through the old plaster when the church added modern air-conditioning.

I look up at the ceiling again. Somehow I've missed the tiny pinholes pushing the cool air into the sanctuary, the pinholes right beside the tiny embedded microphones.

Before Patrick Henry utters his first word, I sprint for the door.

47

It's not the best situation. We are sitting in the white Cadillac with its tinted windows and spoke wheels, parked on East Franklin Street. At night.

Three minutes after John parks, a young guy wearing baggy jeans wanders over, both hands jammed into his front pockets, shoulders hunched like Quasimodo. He passes the car twice with that lope-and-pause walk, acting as though he's not really waiting for us to lower the window and ask for controlled narcotic substances.

I don't want any crack. I want a sweater. Once again, John's car is an arctic freeze.

"You believe my theory?" I ask, teeth chattering.

"*Believe* is a strong word," he says. "But we did find a dead body in the dump. And I am sitting here on Church Hill, for what it's worth. Beats watching the Braves lose."

After my abbreviated visit to St. John's, I raced to John's apartment. Over pepperoni pizza (for me) and beer (for him), I described my visit to LuLu Mendant, his connection to Fielding, my belief that the conversation in the mayor's parlor today was recorded. The padded walls, the soundproof atmosphere, the same high-tech cooling system as St. John's church told me the mayor kept tapes. Why, I didn't know.

But my gut said watching him would tell us more. The dead body wasn't the end of the story; it was a beginning. And John agreed to help, one last time. I knew that pink bicycle call was no impulse. Once upon a time he was a good agent, I know that now.

But the dealer on the corner makes me nervous. "We don't want drugs," I tell John. "So how long before somebody calls the mayor and tells him the cops are parked out here watching his house?"

John doesn't reply. His meaty face stares out the windshield, impassive as granite. I'll bet the wives really appreciated that profile. Finally, he says, "You pray, right? Ask that God of yours to help us out here."

I don't bother telling him that's exactly what I've been doing for the past fifteen minutes, shivering and reminding the One Who Needs No Reminding that when Phaup returns and discovers all this rule bending and wasted manpower, John will retire, and I'll be in Sioux City processing agent applications, with my mother left to Wally and the Pentecostals.

The knock at the window makes me jump. John's hand immediately goes to his holster. It's quasi-Quasimodo. John touches the door's silver tab, lowering the window two inches. I can see the guy's eyes, narrow and bloodshot. They roam the vehicle's interior, searching for information.

"Hey, man, you need directions?"

John slips ten dollars through the window. He says

there's another twenty if some decent Chinese food gets delivered. And if it's the dish with the flapjacks, another ten. Quasi thinks a moment, then pockets the bill. He lopes off toward East Broad Street.

John closes the window. "That buys us thirty minutes."

"How do you figure?"

"I gave him ten bucks, but there's thirty waiting. I know there are no Chinese restaurants on Church Hill because the blacks chased all the Asians out of the neighborhood. So he's got to get to Shockoe Bottom, where he'll ask people who don't speak English about flapjacks. They're Chinese pancakes, not flapjacks, and then he has to wait while they make the pancakes because most people don't order that dish. Then he's got to get back up here for the rest of the money."

"Nice going." My voice is full of appreciation.

"But thirty minutes probably won't make much difference."

Optimism being a Christian duty, I want to argue with him. But I'm too busy watching a lean figure turn the corner off 24th and head down East Franklin, straight for the Mendant circus tent. Under each streetlight, the figure becomes more familiar until he's standing under the gaudy globe outside Mendant's yellow door.

Mel.

"That's the kid from the gym," I tell John. "The fibers I took off the wall? They matched his sweat suit."

John looks over. "You're positive?"

I've seen Mel nearly naked. "Positive."

The bright yellow door opens, and Mel steps inside.

249

No introductions, no questions. There's a long silence in the Cadillac, just the roar of the air conditioner. John asks, "You prayed?"

I nod slowly.

"Nice going," he says.

———•———

Seventeen minutes later, Quasi returns with the Chinese flapjacks, along with his phone number in case we want to order more food at extortionary prices. John hands him the promised money, then carefully places the white takeout bags on the backseat floor. He doesn't eat in the car.

"Drive," I say.

"You're that hungry?"

"Drive!" I point out the windshield. Mel is jumping off the blue steps, landing on the sidewalk, running in the direction he came from. He glances nervously over his shoulder at us, and John shoves the gear. We squeal down East Franklin, following Mel's wiry frame to the corner. He turns north, and John pulls alongside him, sliding down the tinted window. "Want a ride?"

Mel takes off.

John hits the brakes. My door is already open, but Mel's got twenty paces on me. He darts into a narrow alley between Franklin and Broad, and I watch his blade-thin body disappear into the dark. The alley is barely lit by one security light over a dilapidated garage. I creep forward, staying to the edges, then suddenly catch sight of Mel again, this time rounding a trash can. I run. But he's gone. I look up and down 25th.

Mel is a block ahead. I start after him just as the church bells at St. John's ring in midnight. He sees me, turns once, darts south down Broad Street. I'm hoping John's covered that end of the block. But Mel takes one smooth leap over the cemetery wall into St. John's property. The last bells chime. I slow down, knowing the only way out of that cemetery is the way in. The walls are even taller on the other sides, and so old they're worn smooth, impossible to climb solo. I search the street for John, then pull my cell phone from my belt clip. John's number is busy. Great. I leave a message, whispering my location and advising, "Do not call. Hurry."

At the cemetery gate, I wait, hoping John comes to the rescue. When he doesn't, I climb the wrought-iron fence, landing on the other side, pressing my torso into the herringbone brick. Behind me, a city bus groans down East Broad Street. Wishing for my weapon, I clutch my cell phone.

The worm's-eye view shows all the lumpy graves and eroded headstones. In the middle, a big marble crypt packed with First Families of Virginia is half lit by a security beam triggered by Mel's movements.

I creep toward the stones. "Mel, it's the FBI. We want to talk to you."

Adrenaline pumps my veins, and my skin tingles. Staying in the light's shadow, I clasp my hands around my phone, pretending it's a gun, pointing my index fingers. "Mel, come on out. Or I'll have to shoot." I step across a soft berm at the edge of the yard. "I know Hamal was your friend." I scan the decaying stones standing rigid as hostages. "I'm sorry you had to see him die."

251

Light throws shadows behind the old headstones, long black rectangles that look like the ground is opening for fresh graves. I stumble, catch my balance. Where is John? I don't have a weapon, and Mel is full of the supernatural rush of being hunted. Leaning back, I rest against the cemetery wall, that one-word prayer circling my brain: *Please.*

This comes back: *You know this boneyard.*

I start at the far end, examining each headstone, eliminating those too small or eroded to disguise a man. When I get to the crypt, I shuffle to the right, "weapon" poised. Mel holds still as the stones. But angles are amazing things, and when you're playing hide-and-seek, angles work for the seekers. Moving two degrees at a time, I finally sight the white toes of Mel's tennis shoes poking from the bottom of the crypt. Two more degrees, I see his long face pressed against the alabaster marble. He is looking for me. But he can't see me, while I'm looking right at him.

I lower my voice to deep growl. "Get on the ground, Mel, or I'll shoot."

He spins. I raise my "weapon."

"Down or I blow your head off!"

He falls on the grass. "Don't shoot!"

"Hands behind your head!"

Both hands fly up, laced behind his head so fast it's a blur. I walk slowly toward him, keeping the "weapon" poised.

He turns his head, cheek on the grass. "I didn't kill nobody!" he tells me. "I didn't kill nobody."

252

48

Mel seems to explode with God's gift to law enforcement—the urge to confess.

But I want to silence him. In my official low-octave voice, I order him to stop talking. Anything he says now cannot be used against him in a court of law because the FBI agent who collared him is so very suspended she's carrying an imaginary gun. And if Mel speaks now, he could lose the urge to speak later. Pressing my left foot between his shoulder blades, keeping him from seeing my hands, I stare at his bony shoulder blades poking his T-shirt like broken plates. When John finally arrives, ripping his polo shirt as he climbs over the wrought-iron gate into the cemetery, he is cursing. By the time he reaches us, he is a frightening sight—a large angry man one beat from a massive heart attack. Mel takes one look and starts babbling all over again. John listens, breathing heavily, cuffing Mel's wrists behind his back. He rolls him over, pats him down for weapons, then sets Mel's back against the crypt. Actually, Mel pushes himself to the crypt, putting space between himself and John. In the bright security beam, Mel's pulse throbs through his neck's carotid artery. His short hair glistens with sweat.

"It's going to be all right," I tell him.

The expression on his long face is bald desperation, as though I said, "You're cooked, buddy."

For the fifth time, Mel says, "I didn't kill nobody." His voice is high, girlish.

"Who . . ." John is still trying to breathe. "Who . . . didn't you kill?"

"Nobody. I didn't kill nobody. Swear to God."

Swear to God. I know what that means. "So what exactly happened on that roof?" I ask. The urge to confess doesn't always mean immediate truth.

"I didn't mean to kill nobody."

Just what I thought. *Swear to God* is a giant red flag. I keep my voice calm. "You didn't *mean* to kill anybody, or you didn't kill anybody?"

His scared eyes dart from me to John, then back to me, the good cop. "It all happened so fast, it was just crazy, they started yelling at each other and I reached up and—" He drops his head, hands cuffed behind him, his back pressed against the crypt. He looks like a figure from the Inquisition.

"Then what?" John growls.

"They fell."

I look at Mel's young face. I see the fear, the regret. There is no defiance. Only guilt.

"They fell," I repeat. "You watched them fall. Then you pulled yourself over the ledge and took off."

When he doesn't answer, John repeats my question. Mel simply nods. Behind us, I hear car doors slamming

254

on Broad Street, red lights whipping through the night air. Here come fresh horses to spirit our suspect away.

I kneel next to Mel. "You kept one arm in that capstone, deep into the building. And you hung there until Hamal could get the detective on the roof."

"I didn't want to kill nobody," he mumbles.

"I believe you."

John leans down, lowering his voice. "Raleigh, you better take off. I'll handle it from here."

But it's ask now or forever hold my peace. And I'm probably the only person who believes this next question is key. I crouch lower, keeping out of sight of the men who struggle at the cemetery gate. "Did Hamal ask you to kill the detective? Or the girl?"

He turns his head away, his long dark neck graceful as a swan.

"Look at me, Mel."

His brown eyes are molten pools of despair. "She told on him. That detective was going to put him in jail." Tears streak the dark hollow cheeks, landing on the grass like damaged dew. "Hamal said I had to, he said the police were gonna get him."

I look at John; he tosses his head toward the gate. Here come the agents. Crossing the other side of the crypt, I move deep within the shadows, disappearing into a graveyard where the stones are so old the dates no longer matter.

49

The blind woman's half-painted house is still the brightest spot on Ludlow Street. And today, her Astroturf stoop has been hosed clean of city soil; Miss Williamson has been anticipating my visit. She sits behind the iron bars that cover her front door, her callused brown fingers brushing the red leather Bible, turning the Braille into soft, worn paper. Before I take the first porch step, she unlatches the lock on the iron bars.

"I'm so glad you decided to come back," she says. Cat and onion odor wafts out. She looks past me, her eyes clicking across the street. "You didn't bring your friend?"

"No, ma'am."

"What a shame." She locks the iron bars behind me. "I was hoping to sow another seed in that man's heart. He's close, I feel it. That man is so close to breakin' for the Lord."

"Yes, ma'am. You might be right."

She offers me iced tea, and we sit on her plastic-covered couch. Her home is without mess or clutter. I'm guessing there are no cats, that this is the odor of a small Southern home without air-conditioning, a swelter trapped between thin walls and old carpet and fear of the outside.

I open my bag, searching. Early this morning, I walked through the carriage house, collecting my notes for John. The case belongs to him now, and he won't be asking for any declinations. In the first notebook, from that first day here on Ludlow Street, I found the blind woman's statements. This time, her words stopped me cold.

"Miss Williamson, tell me again what you heard," I say. "Tell me about the screams."

The gelatinous eyes quiver toward me. "Everybody and their uncle is callin' me an old fool. But I know what I heard."

"How many screams?"

"Three. I heard those three screams. Almost sounded like four, if you was counting the one that came later."

Before the bodies landed. But right after they fell. Mel's last scream.

"The first two screams, what did they sound like?"

"Well, the first and last scream was the same person. Pitched like a scared woman. But it wasn't a woman."

"And the others?"

"The two men, falling down."

"Miss Williamson, why didn't you mention this when we were here before?"

"I was trying, but your friend didn't give me a chance to 'splain myself."

She's probably right about that. "Tell me more."

"Well," she says, settling back into the plastic-wrapped couch. "The high scream sounded like a real scared person. Troubled. This was young and troubled. Worse thing to be, if you ask me. All that energy and a mind that won't leave you alone. That's like getting a prescription for pure evil."

I ask whether she can identify that particular scream, whether if she heard it again she could be certain. She raises her face with pride. "You're not driving the same vehicle today."

The Benz is parked across Ludlow, just beyond the black bars of her doorway. "What kind of car do you think it is, Miss Williamson?"

"It's got one of them funny engines. Powerful, but the back end putt-putts, like them old foreign cars. Sounds like the engine runs on beans."

I smile. "You're good."

"You spill a pin cushion, I'll tell you how many pins hit the floor. My hearing's a gift from the Lord. Keeps me safe."

I want to run, tell John this news: you've got a witness. And no defense attorney can rattle this one. But there's no leaving now. Not in the South, where hasty exits offend on a deep personal level. And not with someone who can parse death cries of men falling through thin air.

So we sit in her sweltering living room, sipping the watery iced tea, and before long she takes out the worn red Bible. The binding is broken from so much use, from her long fingers absorbing the wisdom. And rubber bands stretch across the leather cover, holding all that good news in place.

50

John wants me to pick up the records from the medical examiner.

"Are you sure?" I'm holding the cell phone with one hand, driving away from Ludlow Street across the Mayo Bridge into Richmond. The James River rushes below, fulminating with the wash of heavy rains. The swirling noise blows into my open windows. "Don't you want to get the records yourself?"

He's too busy. My heart snaps with envy. Bitterness. Even after getting steeped by Miss Williamson in "Let him who boasts, boast of the Lord," mean thoughts invade my head. I try to push them away, but they press forward: this is my 44, the one everybody told me to close. Now John's too busy pursuing it to pick up death records.

Downtown, I wait in Dr. Bauer's big office overlooking the Richmond Coliseum. She is not immediately available. I scan her bookshelves. They contain riveting titles such as *The Medico Legal Guide to Death and Dismemberment*. Behind her desk, a dry-erase board catalogs all the city's pending cases. Name, Date, Place,

Circumstance. I see "Landfill decomp" up there, without a name. I suspect that's going to change very soon.

When Bauer finally appears, her short blond hair wet and tucked behind her neat ears, she is all gamine intelligence, even cooler than last time. "Pardon the wait," she says. "They brought in a gentleman who'd been in the river five days. It appears his beloved wife went fishing with him and struck his head with a blunt object. I took a shower." She flicks the switch on the light box, slipping in the X-rays so that they're side by side. On the left, she explains, is Cheraine Saunders's dental record from MCV. Two abscessed teeth had been pulled. The right X-ray shows the mouth belonging to the body from the landfill. She points at the rectangular hole in the upper left gum. "Further, both X-rays document a broken bicuspid, right there. My dental expert vetted this already. I've enclosed his name for your records."

"We appreciate it."

"Good. The nail polish tests out as the same batch in the bottle. Not as precise as dental records, but it all helps build a case. What was it called?"

"The polish?"

She nods.

"Cherry Dreams. But not anymore."

She raises a perfect eyebrow.

"Her mother called her 'Cherry,'" I explain. "But she won't be dreaming anymore."

Bauer yanks the X-rays from the light box and slides them into a large manila envelope. She hands it to me. "Don't personalize these things," she says. "You'll live to regret it."

When I get to John's condo, his white hair looks like a throw pillow losing its stuffing. But his blue eyes are lit from within—clear, luminous as cut gems. I don't see any beer bottles.

After handing him the dental records from Bauer, along with my notebook from that first day, I explain that the blind woman can identify Mel's scream, if they need her. Then I give him the file from Detective Greene.

"What's this?" he asks.

"That's the cold case on the first Saunders girl. And a boy they never identified. It's what the detective was trying to close when he died." I remind him that Hamal Holmes paid for the girl's funeral, that he made a family with the sister, who is the same girl we just found in the landfill. "It's all weirdly connected."

"Yeah? It gets weirder. Your buddy Charlie Reynolds is writing up search warrants. We're serving tomorrow morning." The boxing gym first, he says, because Mel claims Holmes kept a weapon in his desk. "It's a .38. Who knows, maybe Holmes was careless enough to keep the weapon instead of tossing it. And we'll have his DNA now."

I give him a rundown on Hamal Holmes, the mental instability, what Ray Frey told me about the trip to Atlanta, the Coretta Scott King poisoning. And maybe, just maybe, a twisted sense of duty toward his victims. A mercenary who occasionally succumbed to mercy, even for the people he thought his city was better off without.

"Did Mel explain the plan for the roof?" I ask.

261

"Take out the detective." He shrugs. "But the detective wasn't meeting Holmes. He planned to see the sister up there, the one we found in the landfill. But Holmes knocked her off before she could spill every gruesome detail. Apparently she told the detective enough for him to piece some things together. But for all we know, more bodies are deeper in that landfill."

And now I know a deeper reason behind the city's silence, why no witnesses would come forward that fateful Saturday. Why nobody will talk to the cops about certain cold-case murders. Hamal Holmes, the crack-addicted boxer who turned his life around, the city's crusader for youth on the streets, the man whose gold crucifix sits in a plastic bag in the Bureau's vault—he was methodically, murderously cleansing his beloved Richmond. Junkies and drug dealers, pedophiles and prostitutes carrying AIDS, Holmes made them go away. Perhaps for money, perhaps at somebody's request.

But his crusade carried the mercenary's strange notion of mercy: he paid for their funerals.

"So that's why the detective didn't pull his weapon," I say. "He was expecting the sister."

He nods. "He goes to the roof, and Holmes is there instead, hiding behind the roof door. And Mel's crawled down to that cornice, one arm stuck in that hole where you found that red leather fiber—it's from his boxing glove. He said he put the glove on one hand so the brick wouldn't tear up his fingers." When Holmes pushed the detective into the corner, Mel was supposed to reach up with his open hand and yank the man over the side. "By the time Falcon hit the ground, those two clowns would be long gone."

262

"Only it didn't work that way."

"Neither of those geniuses realized how tired Mel would get hanging off that wall. And the detective was smart. He wouldn't let Holmes move him into the corner. Holmes got turned around."

"Don't tell me."

"Mel pulled his buddy right off the roof."

No wonder he screamed. "But how did the detective fall?"

"Trying to grab Holmes."

"He tried to save him?"

He nods. "He tried to save the guy trying to kill him. And then he fell."

My mind imagines the reaction down at the police department when they hear this. Even more troubling, I consider Janine Falcon's reaction. And then, the other side. "What about LuLu Mendant? Where does he fit in?"

"We're serving him a warrant."

John says the Bureau's white collar investigators were already looking into the mayor, after some tips last year about money laundering and tax evasion. Perhaps some landfill kickbacks. But they couldn't get anything to stick for a warrant. "Until now. He's the real owner of that boxing gym," John says. "And money went through that place on a conveyor belt. They never paid taxes. Go figure."

I tell him my hunch: Fielding got tired of paying off the mayor for his help on city council, so Mendant launched a protest against the hat factory, trying to shame Fielding back into extortion. How convenient to knock off the detective at the same time, when the cop was putting the pieces together.

"Did you find out why Mel went to the mayor's house last night?"

"He claims you stole his sweat suit," John says. "The one he was wearing on the roof. He thought Mendant should know, but somebody called and said we were watching the house. That's when Mel took off running. He won't say much more about the mayor's involvement, but if we find tapes in Mendant's house, it could tell us more." He grins. "Either way, we've got a great case."

I smile, forced. "Congratulations."

He looks at me with an expression I've never seen before on his face. "Raleigh, I need to apologize. You were right. You were right to stick to this case the way you did. I was wrong."

"Thanks." I feel hollow.

"I'll return the favor. I promise. You have my word."

I wave him off, fighting back the bad thoughts. How can he return the favor when he retires in six weeks?

Still smiling, I open the door.

Still smiling, I tell him, "Soak up the glory, John. Go out in a blaze."

I almost mean it.

51

Outside on the street, the night air feels gentle, whispery. But a breeze with bold gusts keeps lifting the tree leaves, revealing silver-green underbellies, warning of an impending thunderstorm. As I walk back to the carriage house, I try to beat back seething self-pity. But it's not a good effort. Phaup suspends me for sticking to the case, and now John is a genius for cracking it. I can already hear the cheers in the office, all the backslapping when John becomes the first agent in Richmond to resolve a civil rights case, not to mention bring down the mayor. It'll be national. He'll retire with honors.

For several long moments, I stand outside my mother's house, staring at Helen's lime green VW Beetle parked at the curb. I let out a groan, then open the kitchen door. My sister sits at the table between Wally and Nadine, while the dog rests at their feet. Nadine wears a Dutch cap and red clogs, like a woman lifted from a Vermeer painting.

"Raleigh!" my mother exclaims. "You're finally home!"

She says it as though she's been waiting a lifetime, as

though I'm the child who never comes around. "Helen is showing us photos of her trip. Come see!"

"How was Amsterdam?" I manage to ask as I slip into a kitchen chair.

"Amazing!" Helen enthuses. "I've been asked to go to Brussels in September. My research on van Gogh is absolutely groundbreaking."

Nadine turns to me, her face shining with joy, cheeks blushing like pink tulips. "Your sister is world famous, Raleigh. Wouldn't your father be so proud?"

I endure fifteen minutes of Helen's photographs. As usual, my sister's made ample use of her camera's self-timer in order to pose in every frame. And why shouldn't she? In addition to everything else, Helen is blessed with a face that looks even better on film. Helen Harmon: her own work of art. Whenever appropriate, I smile. I nod. I oooh and aaah and listen to Helen boast of her brilliance.

Finally, she says, "Let's all go to dinner. My treat."

"Oh yes!" Nadine clasps her hands, the bracelets singing. "Let's go!"

As politely as possible, I decline the invitation, explaining that I have work to do.

"Work, work, work." Nadine scowls. "That's all you do, Raleigh. Why don't you live a little, like your sister?"

Wally quickly says he can't go either, and Helen stands, making a big production that she's getting Nadine out the door in her Dutch gear all by herself, fully insinuating this will be the biggest night in Nadine's life.

Once they're gone, Wally heads to his darkroom, Madame follows him. I cross the slate courtyard, moving through the sensuous Southern evening with heat lightning flashing against the night sky. In the distance, muted thunder grumbles, sounding almost reluctant. I stand at the carriage house windows, waiting for rain. It starts slowly, simple short dances of water. But soon it builds to a roaring crescendo, the rain washing down the brick walls, spilling into the hallowed cobblestone street beyond like a flash flood. When Helen finally returns with Nadine, both of them shriek through the heavy downpour into the kitchen. I turn and walk to my bedroom.

From under the bed, I pull out the shoe box that contains my father's broken Timex. I gather up his legal papers from the other box, all the notes I collected from his desk the day after he died. His blue ink notations still look fresh in the margins. And from a third box, I take out copies of police evidence, laying everything out on the living room floor, fanning it out like a paper quilt. And in the low lamplight, I begin.

I begin to work.

Acknowledgments

No book, particularly one written by a mother with young children, is a solo effort. Without the help of people endowed with generous spirits, this book would not exist. Here are some of the good souls:

The G-men (and women) in the FBI's Richmond field office, who graciously answered my questions. Interviewing these people was nothing short of an honor. In particular, Special Agent Wayne Smith deserves a medal for his tireless support of this project. And Special Agent Katie Land, for her wit. In the Bureau's Materials Analysis Lab, thanks go to Special Agent Bruce Hall, soil specialist extraordinaire, and the hard-working crew in the mineralogy lab.

Richmond is a city full of Southern characters who don't realize they're characters—the best kind—and many are playing within this book. Thanks to all who told me their stories. And the late Nelson Hyde, the character who first opened the door to Richmond.

Detectives Tom Leonard and Boo Quick with the Richmond Police Department let me hang around their shop while they quietly cracked ice-cold cases. Rick Berquist, geologist with the Virginia Division of Mineral Resources, carried soil to my house in a Ziploc bag, then patiently explained why it was special. Amy Brichta, with the Richmond Medical Examiner's office, offered knowledge and scary science books. My agent, Brian Peterson, gave unwavering enthusiasm; my editor at Revell, Lonnie Hull DuPont, graced every step with her poetic spirit. And finally, Rev. Charles "Where's my rock?" Reynolds took me through the book of Micah with piercing intelligence—then said the greatest sentence in the Bible might be "Jesus wept," but a close second is "Jesus laughed."

On a personal note, the wagons gathered many times over the eight years it took to finish this project, allowing me time for interviews and writing. Thanks go to Sherry Clements, who makes kids feel like kings; Pam Hill and her fun house; Claudia Cronin, Crys Gaston, and Robin O'Leary, for friendship beyond measure; Phyllis Theroux, my mentor, my friend; and Debbie Kendrick, who tapped my shoulder one evening many years ago and proceeded to electrify my spirit.

Thanks to my parents, who always encouraged adventure but never forgot what was home. And to all my family in Seattle, especially my brother Roger.

My deepest thanks, however, go to the Three Wise Guys: Joe, Daniel, and Nico. Without your love, laughter, and unending support, this book would not be possible. I am forever grateful.

Sibella Giorello was a features reporter for the *Richmond Times-Dispatch* for more than ten years. Her stories won many state and national awards, including two nominations for the Pulitzer Prize. She now lives in Washington state with her husband and sons. This is her first novel.